THE TIMELESS MOMENT

THE TIMELESS MOMENT

by

Pamela Street

St. Martin's Press
New York

THE TIMELESS MOMENT. Copyright © 1988 by Pamela Street. All rights reserved. Printed in the United States of America. No part of this book may be used or reproduced in any manner whatsoever without written permission except in the case of brief quotations embodied in critical articles or reviews. For information, address St. Martin's Press, 175 Fifth Avenue, New York, N.Y. 10010.

Library of Congress Cataloging-in-Publication Data

Street, Pamela.
        The timeless moment.

        I. Title.
PR6037.T8175T5   1989   823'.914   88-29867
ISBN 0-312-02656-0

First published in Great Britain by Robert Hale Limited.

First U.S. Edition

10 9 8 7 6 5 4 3 2 1

I have never put myself into the charge of the many wheeled creatures that move on rails and gone back . . . lest I might find the trees look small and the elms mere switches and the fields shrunken and the brooks dry, and no voice anywhere – nothing but my own ghost to meet me by every hedge.

Richard Jefferies, *My Old Village*

THE TIMELESS MOMENT

1

Yesterday, I went back to Ivers. I never thought I would, but we were passing so close and, quite suddenly, I heard my voice saying to the driver, 'Would you mind making a small detour? The next turning on the left. There's something I want to look at.'

He seemed surprised, knowing how anxious I had been to get home to Maplethorpe. I was surprised myself, besides being fearful, but Fred was slowing down now and I felt it was too late, as well as rather feeble, to say, 'I'm sorry, I've changed my mind.' Moreover, there was a part of me – the one, perhaps that belonged to an earlier happier past – which still longed to see the place, however much another part of me wished I had never known of its existence.

When we got just short of the village, I asked him to stop and let me out. Then I said, 'If you go on another quarter of a mile or so you'll come to Compton Ivers. Perhaps you would wait for me by the church. I shouldn't be too long.'

'Yes, Mrs Norbury.' I could see from his face that surprise had now given way to genuine curiosity.

I stood there until he was out of sight and then I crossed over the stile and took the right-of-way up Hackpen Hill to Ivers Copse, just as I had done with the Tanner family many more years ago than I cared to remember. Once or twice I paused, partly to get my breath – for I am an old lady now – and partly because I began doubting the wisdom of my unplanned little pilgrimage. But then I plodded on, almost as if on automatic pilot, my legs propelling me forward with a determination all their own.

I climbed a second stile and, for a few yards, plunged into what I recollect the Tanner children – captivated by *The Wind in The Willows* – called the Wild Wood. Overhead, the trees all but blotted out the sky. On either side of me the undergrowth was dense and faintly menacing. I could quite understand why it was here that Caroline, the youngest girl, had slipped her hand into mine. For a short way, all nature seemed to have altered shape and substance and an unpleasant dankness replaced the sweeter smell of the open fields.

Yet, as soon as I came out of the gloom and saw the scene below me, I was glad to have made the effort. It all seemed worth it. I realised I could never have allowed myself to get so near and then given up.

The house, with its grey stone walls and old rose-coloured tiles, lay there in the warm September afternoon looking pleasantly solid and self-contained, just as if it were having a few quiet hours' sun-bathing. On either side, its giant oak trees, with their leaves now turning faintly yellow, seemed to be standing as sentinels, protecting it from any possible intruder, such as myself.

It was all very still, rather like a bright and beautiful stage set. The garden of Ivers was a riot of colour, the field of wheat in the foreground golden and ready for harvesting. Beyond, in the valley, the water-meadows were a mixture of blues and greens and little patches of silver where the river caught the sunlight. Somewhere, down by the mill, amongst a group of willows, there was a cottage I knew – or, rather, knew of – well. Over to my left I could just discern the chimneys of a very much grander establishment, the Hall; and then, a little closer, I could see the squat Norman tower of Compton Ivers church rising as if from a blanket of near-black yew trees.

For a moment, I shut my eyes, but it hardly made any difference. The scene before me was already indelibly etched on my mind. Why had I come there again? I was a fool. There was no need to. If one happened to have a picture-book memory, one could always turn the pages.

I supposed I ought to be getting back to the car. Fred would be wondering what had happened to me. Yet I stayed a little longer, speculating as to who the present owners of Ivers might be. There was really nothing to stop me trying to find out, even calling; but I realised it would hardly be likely that, if they happened to be at home, they would appreciate having their peaceful afternoon interrupted by a strange, ageing female with no entitlement to pay them a visit, other than that once upon a time she was very much involved with the place. Besides, what good would it do? Keep the picture-book permanently open? No, it would be better to go home, to get back to Maplethorpe which held no secrets, had no mysteries and where I felt I rightfully belonged and was safe. As I started off down the right-of-way I thought how good it would be when Fred turned down the lane at Pennyford towards that welcoming little whitewashed house near the Dorset coast.

How many years ago was it that we had rented it as a holiday home for Adam after he had had meningitis? Dear God, it must have been getting on for thirty. And then we had gone on coming every summer even though George, my husband, could never understand the attraction it held for me and our son. He used to say, 'Adam can't possibly want to go there *again*, Vicky. He's growing up. It's such a back-of-beyond place. And you know how difficult it is for me to get away from the Club.'

But I knew Adam *did* want to keep going there. Even though he was still a child, he seemed to have formed a definite attachment to Maplethorpe, just as I had. The nearby farm was a constant source of delight to him, the farmer's children – Sue and Robert Colbert – the brother and sister he had never had. And then there was Herbie. Herbie Ems, the jack-of-all-trades who I swear started my son off on his carving career. One of the best pictures in my mental memory book is of a little boy with fair hair and big brown eyes, holding a penknife and a piece of softwood in his hands, working away at it as he sat on the back step of Maplethorpe for hours on end. I've still got the little rabbit he first made me.

'Damn fool thing to want to take up,' George had said, when he realised Adam was serious about going in for woodwork. 'Why can't the boy do something sensible? He's not going to get far fiddling about with miniature furniture for the rest of his life.'

But I had taken Adam's side. I refrained from pointing out that since George had come out of the army he himself had not exactly gone far. Being secretary of a country club – even if it *was* a very exclusive one, catering for golf and tennis enthusiasts – was not exactly any kind of career, not as far as I was concerned.

Part of Maplethorpe's attraction for me was that it was a refuge from our 'tied' home, where we lived virtually over the shop. Admittedly, our grace-and-favour apartment in one wing was both spacious and comfortable and, if I had preferred it, I need hardly ever have cooked a meal, what with the excellent restaurant immediately below us. But as time went by, I began to look on Ackerley Grange as a kind of prison. I felt it was no place in which to bring up a young child. The atmosphere was rich, rarefied and specious, the clientele sophisticated, the conversation almost entirely confined to the stockmarket, cars, fashion and holidays. I hardly once met a kindred spirit, unless perhaps it was Doctor Kindersley – Sir Derrick, as he later became – to whom I always felt eternally grateful for coming up to our flat and diagnosing Adam's illness the night I had gone down to find George to tell him the child's temperature was 105.

Our son was in hospital most of that summer and, when he was due to come home, it was from Dr Kindersley himself that I first heard about Maplethorpe. He said that some friends of his had a small house in Dorset, ten miles from the sea, which they usually let out at this time of year. Owing to a sudden cancellation he wondered if I would like to take Adam down there to recuperate.

I jumped at the chance. For although the place where we lived was called a *country* club, to my way of thinking this was a misnomer. Plans for a new motorway looked as if it would be coming far too close for comfort. As it was, there was the continual sound of Alfa Romeos and Jaguars revving up in the forecourt. Adam was still very weak. I didn't want him exposed to that kind of life: the stares, the hypocritical female exclamations of 'Vicky darling! How lovely to see you again!' (I had been practically living in the hospital.) 'You must have had such a ghastly time, you poor thing.'

It *had* been a ghastly time, certainly. Only someone who has watched a child battling through a serious illness, knows the agony, the despair, the clinging on to hope which is at its lowest ebb in the early hours of the morning, the faint surge of relief when night is over, the feeling: We've made it. Another day. Maybe all will be well.

Gradually, as the years went by, I swear I began to look forward to our spells at Maplethorpe as much as any child at boarding-school looks forward to the holidays. It became for me an enchanted place, something apart, out of context. The whole vicinity and the inhabitants therein somehow seemed kinder, better. I suppose the people of Pennyford must have had their share of troubles, but I was rarely aware of them. They smiled easily and when it was known – through that swift, mysterious but never-failing method of communication: the rural grapevine – that the Norburys were coming, it sometimes seemed as if there was a reception committee awaiting us as we drove slowly along the village street. 'Hi, Adam!' 'Hello, Mrs Norbury.' 'Lovely weather you've brought.' 'Mrs Markby's got Maplethorpe all ready for you.' Dear Markie, who made life even more pleasant for us.

After that first holiday, when I think George felt I might need some moral support, he rarely came with us or, if he did, he only stayed a night or two. And, of course, to give him his due, summer was the time when he was most busy. He was a good club secretary – 'the colonel', as he was called – convivial and tactful. In his early days in the army he hadn't been an adjutant in a RA regiment for nothing. Ackerley Grange became more and more popular under his care. The fact that he had married a wife who had never been 'good at a party' and had, in fact, gone out of her way to avoid them, must have been a big disappointment to him. The heightened emotions and physical attraction which had brought us together in wartime gradually subsided into a partnership still held together by lingering affection, familiarity and the fact that we were the parents of Adam, who had come along a few years after the war had ended.

In his way, I believe George was as fond of our child as I was, but he wanted him to be someone I knew he could never be, almost from the start. The meningitis, of course, put paid to any athletic prowess he might have shown. He always walked with a slight limp after that. Yet I think this was a relief to the boy, for it meant that his father stopped trying to make him follow in his footsteps. The miniature set of golf clubs he had had specially made for him were put away. Adam was excused soccer and rugby at school. True, he wasn't too bad at cricket and was an excellent wicket-keeper, but that was about as far as it went. All the child's leanings were towards the arts. He read voraciously, appreciated music and produced some well-above average paintings. But it was the wood-carving which really held him. I think at first it was just the feel of the wood in his hands and knowing that he alone could shape it into another form, a beautiful one which appealed to his aesthetic senses and also gave him an awareness of power and security, even peace.

This peace in which to do something creative was a kind of bonus which we shared at Maplethorpe. For it was here that I started to work on my great-grandmother's diaries and when Ivers assumed such importance in my life. My mother had once remarked that she thought they would make an interesting record and, knowing that I had harboured ideas of a journalistic career in my early years, I might like to edit them. At the time I had made it clear that the suggestion did not appeal to me. Looking back, I am sure my reaction must have hurt her. Youth is so incredibly thoughtless.

I was glad that she had still been alive when I began to read them and was able to tell her that I was finding them fascinating. After that first holiday at Maplethorpe when Adam, still weak, took up much of my time, I decided to take the diaries with me in a suitcase, knowing that my child would not need such constant supervision or entertainment. He would be more than happy playing with the Colbert children at Warreners Farm or, as it turned out, picking up some tricks of his trade from Herbie Ems. Not that Herbie went in for any fine carving such as Adam eventually did. But at a young age the child learnt a lot about wood, how to saw it, plane it, polish it and join it together. He helped Herbie to make a low coffee table from some planks of oak that had once spanned a disused ditch in the water-meadows and which I bought to take back to Ackerley Grange with us.

All such memories of Maplethorpe, along with others of Ivers, seemed to jostle for supremacy in my mind on this sunny September afternoon, when I had broken my vow never to go there again. As I began making my way back to Fred and the car, I thought how odd it was that there were these two houses in the English countryside which, in their very different ways, were of so much significance to me: the first, which I now owned and lived in, the second, into whose history I had delved deep and which had helped to make it possible for me to acquire the other. A further point which struck me as I reached the road leading to the village was the fact that I had never cared very much about my predecessors at Maplethorpe, yet perhaps I had cared too much about the earlier inhabitants of Ivers.

I could see Fred standing by the car as I drew nearer the church. He was looking anxiously in my direction. I had employed him to drive me for many years now, whenever I have had any distance to travel on a professional assignment. I believe he looked on his job not merely as a chauffeur but as a guardian. I was aware that I had sometimes alarmed him by trying to fit too much in and trying to get home in the middle of the night because, as the years went by, I became increasingly averse to sleeping out of my own bed. But on the whole I do not think, until today, he had ever considered me fanciful or difficult. Now, however, it was obvious I was falling down on both counts.

'I've been looking at the map,' he said, as he held open the car door and helped me in. 'If we go on we'll hit the main road again in a couple of miles. Save us a bit of time.'

'No, Fred,' I told him firmly. 'I want you to drive back the way we came.'

He stared at me, concern plainly evident in his honest face. It occurred to me that perhaps he thought I was being overtaken by senility.

2

Another year! I can hardly believe Hannah's birthday has come round. She has been a good baby to rear but, alas, she may be my last. Dr Allingham has warned me that a further pregnancy is not advisable and that I should count myself fortunate to be the mother of five healthy girls. He also feels it is possible I may be in for an early Change.

All the same, I wish I could have presented Lionel with a boy. I know how much he would have liked a son to carry on Ivers Farm after him. He does so love the place. Times for farmers are worsening and he is worried the winter wheat is only just showing on Hackpen Hill. He got Widow Shergold's boy to go rook-scaring there on Christmas Day. Little Percy is only ten but his mother has been on Parish Relief, poor thing, ever since Bert Shergold was killed by that fall of chalk in the chalkpit. The Reverend Mr Graham thought it best if Percy left school and so he arranged with Lionel to take the lad on as a bird-starver at a shilling a week. I do hope that won't mean a reduction in poor Sarah Shergold's relief money. She has three other younger children to feed, but the washing and other work she does can't bring in all that much. I have noticed that there is never a light in the cottage come nightfall. I'm glad the Earl of Dewhurst sent her a couple of rabbits on Christmas Eve. If the Poor Law tries to interfere now Percy has become a wage-earner, I shall try to get Lionel to speak to Henry Ponsonby, the Earl's agent, about it. He could then approach Lord Dewhurst, who would surely intervene on the Shergolds' behalf. For all his austere manner, he is a fair man and a more reasonable landlord than most.

I was sitting outside Maplethorpe, working at the rough-hewn garden table – another of Herbie's creations on which Great-grandmother's diaries were spread out before me. It was mid-August, the second time I had rented the place. The evenings were drawing in and Adam was already in

bed and fast asleep, for we had spent a long day at the sea
with the Colbert children and their mother. Now, with my
time to myself, I had lit an old oil lamp and placed it on
one side of the table to assist me with my labours. I thought
what a luxury this would have seemed to Widow Shergold,
who evidently could not afford any form of illumination
once darkness fell.

My light in the garden, of course, attracted the moths.
They came homing in, one particularly large one which
flapped and circled so persistently that, in the end, I
extinguished the lamp and simply sat there, thinking about
Great-grandmother Alice Medway and her sadness at not
being able to present her husband with a son and heir.
And I also thought a lot about Widow Shergold who *had*
produced a son for the unfortunate Bert, and how this
little boy had been forced to start work at the age of ten.

Just before the moths put an end to my reading and
note-taking for the day, I had learned some more about
him: how he could read and write and say his tables before
he had left school. I suspected that he could well have
been better educated at that age than many a child of
today, but it saddened me to think of him standing all
alone in a field on Christmas Day, shaking a tin with stones
in it and probably feeling hungry. For I gathered that my
great-grandmother was worried about what his family had,
or did not have, to eat. She apparently instructed her cook
always to give Percy an apple or a piece of cake when he
came to the back door of Ivers Farm, pushing a wheelbarrow containing the clean laundry over which his mother
had no doubt taken great pains.

Great-grandmother – Alice, or Great-Granny Alice, as I
came to think of her – was obviously a nice woman. She
felt for other people: her husband, her children, Percy
Shergold and the rest of the community in which she lived.
I was not too sure about Great-grandfather Lionel, who had
apparently lashed out with his hunting-crop the previous
October, when he had caught one of his younger employees 'riding the roller' after wheat-sowing on Hackpen
Hill, instead of staggering along beside the horses.

I sat on in the garden at Maplethorpe, the past very

much with me. The air was soft and still, the scent of late-flowering roses almost overpowering. It was a good time for reflection. How happy, I wondered, had Alice been compared, say, to my grandmother (the good baby, Hannah) and my mother and myself? From what did she derive her pleasure? Duty? Acceptance? Motherhood? So far, there was little about actual *love*. Could she have loved the man who had lashed out with his hunting-crop? Surely not. The fact that she had recorded the event at all meant that it must have distressed her. Presumably she did not show Lionel her day-to-day scribblings, as she kept them under lock and key. Were they simply an outlet for her, an escape from that way of life into which God had called her? Did she turn to her diaries as a present-day woman might turn to the bottle or Valium or the psychiatrist's couch? If so, they were certainly a far less expensive and disastrous consolation. Or did Alice really feel she was writing for posterity, that in years to come one of her descendants might find her writings interesting? Perhaps, when I read further, she might let me into her secret. For the moment I just felt grateful that it was I who had been given the privilege of being on the receiving end of a first-hand account of a bygone age.

Suddenly, there was the sound of footsteps in the lane, the lifting of the catch on the garden gate and then Diana Colbert came round the side of the house. She and I had become friends almost as soon as I first came to Maplethorpe, just as our respective children had done the same. She was a tall, dark, striking-looking woman who had been in ENSA during the war and after it had given up quite a promising career as an actress to marry a west-country farmer. She was one of the most uncomplicated people I have ever met. There was a calm about her which I would have given anything to have possessed.

'Hi! Adam left this in my car. I thought he might need it first thing tomorrow. It's nippy in the early mornings now.' She held out his navy-blue sweater.

I thanked her and asked if she would like a drink.

'I wouldn't say "No", that is, if you'll have one too.'

'Of course. I've got a bottle of brandy here which George

insisted we brought with us, for emergencies. This'll be a splendid excuse to open it.'

She laughed. 'Hardly an emergency, but I can't think of anything nicer.'

I went inside and she sat down at the table. When I returned, apologising for the lack of proper brandy glasses, she nodded towards all the papers and books and my clip-board on which I had been making a few notes.

'I didn't like to pry. In any case, the light's not good enough. But are you writing something?'

'No. Not exactly. I'm going through what someone else has written.'

'Anyone you know?'

'No. Although I'm beginning to feel I do. I'm reading my great-grandmother's diaries. She was married to a farmer just like you. They lived not all that far away from here, on the borders of Berkshire and Wiltshire.'

'Really? How perfectly splendid. How far have you got?'

'Well, at the moment I'm completely captivated by 1873 and a little boy called Percy Shergold. I'm afraid I'm not an organised researcher or anything like that. I tend to hop about too much. Something or other catches my fancy and I get stuck. I guess it'll take me a long time to arrange and edit them properly.'

'But one day they'll be published?'

'It would be nice to think so. But I don't like to count my chickens before they are hatched. Just now I'm, well . . . simply enjoying my great-grandmother.'

'And Percy. Tell me about him.'

I told her. The brandy was good – George would have seen to that – and when a small breeze got up I gathered my work together and we went indoors and each had a second glass.

'I wonder,' Diana said at one stage, 'how much we've progressed since those times. Emotionally, that is. Sure, there are no Percys who would be allowed to leave school at the age of ten. And rook-scaring is done by automatic bangers and I don't know anyone in our cottages who sits in the dark because they can't afford a light, although one or two of them still don't have inside sanitation. It's something Edward's hoping to make good by the end of the year. But, just imagine, Vicky. You and I with, say, four or five kids, trying to cope like Widow Shergold. I'd be off my rocker in no time. Behind bars in one of those old-fashioned lunatic asylums that they now call psychiatric hospitals.'

'Yes. Me, too. They had a lot more moral fibre in those days. I suppose Great-Granny Alice would turn in her grave if she could see you and me now, two debauched women drinking alone, rather as I imagine Lionel must have done with one of his male cronies.'

'Yes. But that reminds me. Look at the time. Nearly eleven. Edward will be wondering where the hell I am, although he knows that you and I always have plenty to talk about. But tonight I shall tell him that we were joined by Alice and Lionel and Percy. That'll keep him guessing.'

She got up to go and I came with her to the gate. An embryo harvest moon – still but crescent-shaped – had risen and in its light I watched Diana disappearing up the lane. As I returned to the house the telephone was ringing. It was, as I thought, Edward.

'She's on her way,' I said. 'I'm afraid we got . . . side-tracked.'

He laughed. 'Thanks, Vicky, I'm glad. She enjoys your company. She doesn't get a lot of . . . mental stimulus these days. We're a pretty quiet lot in Pennyford. Ah, here she comes.'

He was obviously relieved. We said goodbye and I went round shutting up for the night. I myself couldn't have enough of the quiet to which Edward referred although I, too, was glad of a friend such as Diana, so different from any of the females I encountered at Ackerley Grange. I felt I should like to stay at Maplethorpe for ever. I was not in the slightest scared of being there alone, especially now Adam was so much fitter. It was a place where I felt nothing bad could ever happen and I believe most of the others in the neighbourhood felt the same. But I realised it had been a bit thoughtless of Diana and me not to think Edward might be a little worried. He was a devoted husband. I did not imagine he would take kindly to his own wife and children going off for several weeks' holiday, as Adam and I did. But then George and I have a different relationship. I suppose ours isn't all that bad a marriage, as marriages go. But we haven't much in common, now the sex thing is on the wane. Much of our trouble, I expect, stems from the fact that, for the life of me, I've never been able to take to club life, whereas Diana, even though a town girl, took to farming like the proverbial duck to water. I felt she could easily have been a present-day Alice, with her kindness and generosity of spirit, although she certainly didn't have a husband such as Lionel to contend with. But she even looked much more like my great-grandmother than I did. From the one faded sepia photograph I had of Alice, she was a tall dark statuesque woman with a gentle, open, yet somehow noble face. She was not a bit like I am: small and thin and mousy-haired, given to introspection and a desire to over-protect my son, especially since he had meningitis.

As I drifted off to sleep that night, I kept thinking about heredity and all the characteristics which are handed down from generation to generation. If I was not like Alice then who did I take after? Please God, not Lionel, but I mustn't forget that males have just as much responsibility when it comes to genetic constitution. But surely, I thought, Adam has taken after me? I can see nothing of George in him whatsoever.

In my dreams I somehow muddled up Percy and Adam and was glad when morning came that I wasn't having to send my son bird-starving on Hackpen Hill.

3

One summer, just after we returned to Ackerley Grange from Maplethorpe, my mother became ill. She was then living in a small flat at Chiswick to which, as I now see it, I had 'bundled' her immediately after my father's death. In my desire to get her reasonably settled within striking distance of my own home and where, mistakenly, I thought she would be able to forge a new life for herself, I realise I acted with unseemly haste and little imagination. I saw her situation through *my* eyes and made no attempt to see it through hers. Having never been bereaved of a husband myself and also being twenty-five years younger, just why I should have thought I knew best has constantly both surprised and distressed me.

I had never had what I would call a close relationship with either of my parents. My father was a market gardener, inheriting the business from his own father. Before her marriage when she was already past thirty – rather late in those days – my mother had taught English at a girls' public school. I often speculated as to just why she married at all, for she was not a passionate woman and it was difficult to think of her as being in love. But then, perhaps, it is always difficult for any child to appreciate what his or her parents were like in their younger days and the forces which drew them together. I suppose my mother could have wanted children but, once established in a large red-brick Victorian house on the outskirts of Canterbury, where she quickly proceeded to give birth to my brother and myself, I think she came to feel trapped. At least, that is the impression she always gave me. There was not enough money to employ resident help, for although my father knew a great deal about flowers and vegetables, he knew precious little about accounts. He was tall, thin and fair – not unlike Adam – with, about him, a permanent aura of vagueness. Or maybe it was just that his concentration went so much on carnations and carrots that there simply wasn't a lot left over for family and friends.

Not that he actually neglected us. He was kind, but in

a distant way, giving the impression that he liked having us around and genuinely wanted us all to be happy. I can quite understand how he must sometimes have driven my mother to distraction. She was the active one. Indeed, she had to be. And she was intensely ambitious for us children. Frustrated that marriage and motherhood had ended her own career, she was extremely anxious that nothing should interfere with that of my brother, Howard, and my own. She wanted us to have every opportunity of getting to the top. That the war brought Howard's law studies to an end and the Battle of Alamein brought about his death was something she never got over.

As for me, she realised that any attempts at a career, such as journalism, would have to be abandoned until hostilities were over and she accepted the fact that I would have to do war work of some kind. She was delighted when the authorities told my father that, if and when conscription for women was brought in, I would be exempt from joining any of the services, so long as I remained at home helping in the nurseries, which would have to be turned over completely to producing food for Britain, an island nation now almost totally dependent on its own resources. Sadly, for her, I had other ideas.

The night before I was due to report to Aldermaston in the summer of 1940 as a private in the ATS, my mother came and sat on my bed. Howard was already at an officer cadets' training unit on Salisbury Plain. All England was waiting for Hitler to 'come on over' after our retreat from Dunkirk. Churchill had given a warning that the Battle of Britain was about to begin and, that very day, the first dog-fight between Spitfires and Messerschmitts had taken place in the skies above our home. Here was I, going off to the comparative safety of the Berkshire countryside and distressing two people who had, after all, brought me up to the best of their ability, sheltered me, clothed me, sat up at night with me when I suffered from bronchitis as a child and were asking no more than that I should stick out the war with them. At least, they didn't actually ask, but I knew what was in their minds. I may have been about to join the army, but I felt a deserter.

It soon became clear that my mother had evidently considered it necessary to take it upon herself to give me some kind of talk before I left the family nest. She seemed reluctant and embarrassed.

'You'll write often, as often as you can, won't you, Vicky. Keep in touch. I hope you find your new life comes up to expectations. It's bound to be very different. I dare say there will be dangers.'

'How do you mean? It seems you and Father are in more danger here at the moment.'

She looked away. I noticed how grey her hair had become at the temples. There were crow's feet near her eyes that I could have sworn had not been there a year before.

'I wasn't meaning that kind of danger,' she replied.

I stared at her. I was nineteen and as innocent as they come. Then the penny dropped.

'Oh, I see. You mean me. The licentious soldiery.' To hide my own embarrassment and unease, I became facetious.

'Yes. You're a lovely girl, Vicky. You could be taken advantage of.'

'Don't worry, Mother. I'm sure I know how to take care of myself. And remember the authorities are pretty strict. I believe the ATS officers work us like demons. They won't stand any nonsense.'

'I should like to think you'll end up an officer yourself.'

'That's in the lap of the gods. I just intend to do my bit.'

As soon as I had uttered the words, I regretted them. She knew and I knew my 'bit' would have been of far more value if I had stayed at Greenways Nurseries.

After she had said good night, I found it impossible to sleep. In any case, the wail of an air-raid siren in Canterbury sounded loud and clear and, miserably, I joined my parents in the cellar below our house. 'It's the glass,' my father kept saying. 'God knows how all the Greenways' glass is going to escape.'

The next morning, having made a quick inspection and found to his relief that all was well, he abandoned his usual duties and, rather to my surprise, accompanied my mother to see me off at the station. I waved to them out of the carriage window as long as it was possible and then sat back with a kind of guilty thrill, listening to the sound of the train carrying me forward to what was to be a life of excitement, weariness, responsibility and, eventually, marriage to George.

I don't think my mother ever took to him, but she did her best. As for George, he simply looked upon her as a mother-in-law whom he found pleasant enough, did not interfere and whom he was quite willing to see at infrequent intervals, when they would engage in conversation which I believe he found a little tedious and somewhat above his level. Occasionally, to lighten these, he would make a few jokes – never in the slightest bit risqué – at which my mother would laugh, hopefully. But I was always glad when such meetings came to an end. I suspect it was a relief all round although, when my father had been alive, George would sometimes inveigle him out for a drink at our local pub or insist on taking us all to some nearby hotel which provided, in those days, the statutory five-shilling dinner, at which my husband made an excellent host.

As time passed and the war ended and later on my mother became a grandmother, I noticed that there was an ever-widening gulf in my relationship with her, but an ever-growing closeness between her and my son. She doted on Adam. Her great joy was to be allowed to have him for a weekend with her at Chiswick or to come herself to Ackerley Grange for a day - though never longer. She was quite adamant about not stopping a night. I think she felt out of her depth and the ambience unnerving. Therefore, when old age and illness crept up on her and she told me it would be necessary for her to go into hospital for an operation, I was not surprised when she categorically refused my suggestion that she should convalesce at Ackerley.

What I *was* surprised about and simply hadn't bargained for was George's reaction, when I told him of both my invitation and her rejection of it.

'But Vicky. You should never have asked her. There could be no question of her coming here.'

'Why not? It's the least I could do. I'm all she has in the world now, at least who can *do* anything. Her brother and sister are both dead. Neither had offspring.'

He was strangely angry, angrier than I had ever known him. 'Don't you realise the authorities have stipulated that no dependants, other than children, can occupy our flat?'

'But she wouldn't be *occupying* it. Just spending a holiday with us until she gets over the operation.'

'And who's to say how long that will take? Or even if she *will* get over it.'

I said nothing, amazed at his matter-of-fact callous reply.

'You've said the operation is exploratory,' my husband continued. 'It seems obvious to me that she has . . . cancer.' He seemed to have difficulty in actually bringing out the word. 'Cancer of the stomach at her age could be . . . well, let's face it, Vicky . . . pretty nasty. I believe there are some excellent convalescent homes on the south coast. You must enquire about them.'

So I did. Or, rather, I asked for a private appointment with the specialist who was dealing with my mother's case.

He was quite sympathetic. I suppose doctors are used to spouses whose opposite numbers cut up rough about relatives of the other side, as it were. It was a situation I myself had somehow never envisaged. Now it was upon me with all its hideous repercussions: a new, unexpected, kind of estrangement between my husband and myself; a sick, possibly dying mother; my own inadequacy; the checking of my personal finances so that at least I could buy the comfort which I, alone, would have freely given; the knowledge that my mother's independent and undemanding streak would make her difficult to handle and, lastly, that I could never measure up to the qualities of my ancestors, particularly the woman whose diaries I was reading: Great-Granny Alice.

4

Today I left Hannah in the care of Ethel, the nursemaid, and got Shiner to drive me and the other four girls over to Ditchington in the pony and trap to see their grandmother. I fear that our visit may have been too much for her. She looked tired and drawn when we left. Before our departure, I managed to take Miss James, her companion, aside and asked her to send me word immediately if she notices further signs of deterioration in Mamma's health. I wonder, perhaps, whether senility might be creeping on. She asked three times where Hannah was and why we had not brought her too. When I explained that it would not have been wise to bring the baby four miles in the trap, especially in this unexpected heat, she seemed quite put out and accused me of keeping the children from her.

I shall have a long talk to Lionel about Mamma when he is in a good mood. We are, of course, fortunate in having the services of Miss James, but I think she is going through the Change. She was red-faced from the neck up and appeared flustered throughout our entire visit, rather like an anxious turkey-cock. If she cannot fulfil her duties, then I should like to have Mamma here. We could easily turn the sewing-room next to the pantry into a ground-floor bedroom and Miss Clutterbuck could use the old scullery each week when she comes to do the mending. The paraffin heater warms the place quite adequately, so long as the housemaid lights it at six-thirty that morning.

Quite a woman, I thought, was Great-Granny Alice. She may have had a difficult husband, but she evidently knew how to handle him. I felt she was much more practised in women's wiles than I was. Whatever opposition Lionel might have put up to having his mother-in-law installed at Ivers, I was sure that my great-grandmother would have got her way. Moreover, I sensed that she would have still managed to keep the household running 'suently', that west-country expression for 'easily' or 'on oiled wheels', which I had noted cropped up in her diaries more than once. Whereas I, confronted nearly a hundred years later with a somewhat similar problem to Alice's, felt I had no chance of standing up to George's laying down of the law. (I was not to know until later that the stand he had taken was due to his pathological fear of cancer.)

My mother went into a private room - this I managed to insist upon – in a West London hospital the first week in October. I went to see her the day after her operation and the Sister called me into her office before my visit.

'Mrs Norbury, I feel I should warn you. Your mother has had a colostomy.'

'A colostomy?' I frowned. We were into the 'sixties, but the word was scarcely part of my vocabulary. I vaguely knew that it was some kind of by-pass of the bowel, but the technicalities were not the kind on which I wished to dwell.

'She has to wear a bag at the moment,' the Sister continued. She was a bright, breezy woman, whom I judged to be my junior by a good ten years or more.

'A bag?' I enquired, in a parrot-fashioned unintelligent way.

'Yes. For the disposal of faeces, you understand. In some cases it is possible that a second operation can be performed so that elimination can revert to the normal outlet. Mr Steiner is not yet certain whether this can be achieved in your mother's case. What was to have been an exploratory operation proved to be something bigger and far more urgent than anyone envisaged.'

'You mean . . . she might always have to have artificial means . . .' I couldn't go on.

She looked at me more kindly. 'Yes.'

I stared down at the floor: brown linoleum and bilious-looking green walls, even though it was the private sector. My mother, so clean, so fastidious, having to have this method of defecation for the rest of her life? Suddenly, Great-Granny Alice came into my mind. Nothing like this would have happened in her day. People may have suffered pain, but wasn't it better? Better to have snuffed out

more quickly without the humiliating degrading business
of having a waste disposal unit affixed to their stomachs?
Pain, in Alice's day, was accepted as part of the human
lot. It might crucify or ennoble, but it wasn't swept under
the carpet, held at bay by tranquillisers and other artificial
means, so that people went on living half-lives in a terrible
twilight world.

Was that why the young of today, I wondered, craved
stimulus? Deprived of natural pain, perhaps they needed
loud music, anything to shock or give them a sensation.
The Beatles had just come on to the scene and it struck me
that twenty years ago these young men might well have
got their kicks in the skies above Canterbury. But then I
chided myself for such thoughts. The war, thank God, was
over. It had been ghastly. So much pain, physical and
emotional. Surely I wasn't advocating suffering, was I?
And all good doctors were dedicated to alleviating it and
to prolonging life to the best of their ability. The surgeon
in charge of my mother's case had seen fit to fix her up in
this manner and, who knows, perhaps he *would* be able to
perform a second operation and return her to the status
quo. I must hope, give *her* hope.

It was unfortunate that when I went along the passage
and found Room 8 there was an *Engaged* notice hanging
on the door. Even more unfortunate when it opened and
a young nurse came out pushing a trolley on which I
could only assume, judging by the smell, was some soiled
equipment. Once I was allowed into the room, the smell
seemed worse, for the windows were closed and a feeling
of nausea welled up inside me. It was all I could do not to
back out or at least throw open a window. Mustering all
my courage, I advanced towards my mother's bed.

She lay with her eyes closed, her face grey and slack.
She was not asleep but she was unaware of my presence.
I suspected that whatever ministrations to which she had
just been subjected had both exhausted and distressed
her. I sat down in the one easy chair, although I would
dearly have loved to return to the waiting-room for a
while.

Presently, my mother opened her eyes and stared at me,

blankly. Then she said, 'How long have you been here, Vicky?'

'About ten minutes.'

'They've told you, have they?'

I parried a little. 'About the operation?'

'About the . . . about what I have to wear.' She evidently found it difficult to say 'bag', just as George had found it difficult to say 'cancer'.

'Yes,' I answered.

'I don't want it, Vicky. I don't want to live like this.'

'But let's hope you won't have to, Mother. Mr Steiner can probably do another op and make you . . .' This time, I hesitated. I had been going to say 'as good as new', but seeing the defeated look in her face, her thin bony arms lying quite still on either side of her body, I knew she would never be that again. 'Just as you were,' I ended up, rather lamely, thinking that it sounded a little less hearty.

This time a kind of blaze came suddenly into her eyes. Almost, she hissed at me. 'I tell you, Vicky, I don't want a second operation. I want to die.'

'Don't say that, Mother. Please. You've always said how much you want to see Adam grow up. You'll feel quite different in a day or two, I'm sure. You wait. I'll come every day. Around this time.' I looked at my watch. The Sister had warned me not to stay too long today. In any case, I had to pick up Adam from school. By rights – or what George felt would have been right – he should have been away at prep school now, but the child's illness had at least lent valid support to my argument for keeping Adam at home until he went to public school, even though, paradoxically, I could have wished that home was a more suitable one.

I got up. The voice from the bed was weak but quite definite. 'I am no good to Adam now, Vicky. There was a time when I felt . . . my influence . . . might have helped. But I would not want him at Chiswick any more. It would not be . . . seemly.'

The last word seemed to come straight from Great-Granny Alice's diaries. 'Seemly', 'suently'. Here was my mother coming out with one of them as if she might have been that venerable lady herself.

'We'll see about that, Mother,' I said, as I leant over and kissed her. 'You're bound to feel wretched for a while. But it won't last. You'll soon be looking on the bright side again.'

I left her, promising to return the following day, amazed and somehow ashamed at my ability to pretend to a confidence I did not really feel.

I managed to visit my mother every day while she was in the London hospital, but when they moved her to a nursing-home near Hayward's Heath, I went every other day. Mr. Steiner told me that he would re-assess her case after she had been at The Laurels a month, a month which began with her appearing to be as low mentally as physically.

It occurred to me when driving down there during the second week that some kind of interest in things outside herself might be kindled if I talked to her about Alice's diaries and the work I was doing on them which I found fascinating. At first, I got little response, but one day when I mentioned that her own mother, Hannah, had apparently been the beauty of the family, she said, 'Yes, she was. Very beautiful.' But then, unfortunately, she went on to add the rider, 'She was never an ugly sick old woman, like Adam will remember me.'

'Don't be silly, Mother.' I spoke quite sharply now. Hitherto, she had never shown a self-pitying streak. 'Why ever should Adam think that? He remarked only the other day that you had never gone grey. I told him all the Medway women were fortunate like that. Now, tell me more about Hannah as a young girl.'

There was a pause while my mother seemed to be cogitating. Then she said, 'She was much more light-hearted than I am. Of course, being the baby of the family, she got rather spoiled. She was always Lionel's favourite. He was a difficult husband, as you must have gathered by now, but Hannah could twist him round her little finger.'

'Great-Granny Alice wasn't bad at that either,' I remarked.

For the first time since her operation, my mother gave a

slight smile. 'Yes. They were well matched. I don't recall if it's in the diaries, but Lionel was a bit of a gambler though never on the horses. Apparently later on in their marriage, he got it into his head that he would like to go to Monte Carlo. Farming must have perked up a bit by then. But can you imagine it? A tenant farmer in those days going off to Monte. Alice said he couldn't go unless he took one of his daughters with him, so naturally he chose Hannah even though she was only about fifteen. The idea was that they were to go on into Italy to improve Hannah's education. Well, that was put about as the ostensible reason for the trip. But Lionel went and lost all their travelling money in Monte and had to wire back to Ivers for enough to get home. Poor Hannah never even crossed the Italian border. I gather that Lionel never looked at a pack of cards afterwards. Alice saw to that.'

It was quite a long speech, certainly the longest my mother had made during her illness. It made me realise two things: one was that I had hit on exactly the right means of taking her out of herself and wondered why I had not thought of it before; the other, purely self-interested and therefore far less commendable: if I was really serious about producing a book based on Great-Granny Alice's diaries, it would be only sensible to glean as much as I could about my predecessors from the lips of someone whom I feared might not have long to live.

5

Since Mamma has come to live at Ivers, she has formed a great attachment to Miss Clutterbuck. I have therefore engaged her to spend every week-day afternoon here from two until four, at threepence an hour. She carries whatever mending there is to be done into Mamma's room and hardly uses the old scullery at all, except for big jobs such as turning sheets sides to middle with the new sewing-machine. Such a wonderful invention. I cannot think how we got on at all without Mr Singer.

Because of this new development in our household, I have told Mrs Graham, the Rector's wife, that I would be quite willing to let the jumble accumulate in the old scullery until the August Bank Holiday fête. She was delighted. It means that she and I and Miss Clutterbuck can go through it at our leisure. Lady Dewhurst has already sent down some excellent articles. There is a good pair of boots which undoubtedly belonged to her second son and which I am sure will just fit Percy. When the poor boy came to the dining-room window to collect his wages along with the other men last Friday, I noticed from the summer-house that he was hobbling. I suspect the soles of his own boots are quite worn through. If the Rector's wife agrees, I will buy the Dewhurst boots and give them to Widow Shergold. We should probably have priced them at sixpence three-farthings, or thereabouts, so I think it would be only fair for me to put a little more than that into the kitty, say sevenpence half-penny, as I would not like anyone to feel I am taking advantage of my position.

Good old Alice. Probably a staunch Tory with a Socialist's heart. Although, of course, I suddenly remembered that there weren't such people as Socialists in those days. Keir Hardie and the Labour Party were yet to come. I said something of this sort to my mother. We were sitting in the conservatory at The Laurels, because there was an Indian Summer that year. She actually laughed.

'I dare say you're right, Vicky. Except you must also remember that a lot of *noblesse oblige* went on at that time.'

'Good thing, too. I'd say Great-Granny Alice was a very happy woman, wouldn't you, doing her stuff in that state of life into which it had pleased God to call her.'

'Yes, and my mother inherited the same attribute. Hannah wasn't as . . . well . . . as *worthy* as your great-grandmother, if you see what I mean. She was too scatter-brained, but she was a very loving, tender-hearted mother. I remember how she used to come and sing to us as children whenever we had toothache. *Where My Caravan Has Rested*. Songs such as that. She was like a pretty little doll perched on the end of my bed. I'm afraid . . .' She faltered and then went on, 'Well, I've always felt I had so many shortcomings as a mother.'

'Rubbish! You've been a very good one,' I broke in quickly, too quickly, perhaps. 'And I really don't think I'd have liked a pretty little doll singing on my bed.'

'No? Well, possibly not.'

'Was my grandfather as difficult as Great-grandfather Lionel?' (I had never known either of my maternal grandparents as, sadly, they had been killed in an accident before I was born.)

'Heavens, no. He was gentle, kind. I expect that was what made me marry your father because he took so much after my own.'

'I see.' I was beginning to think I saw a lot. My mother had wanted to repeat the happiness she had known as a child – and failed. What was more she *knew* she had failed. Perhaps that was why she set such store on her relationship with my son.

'Adam takes very much after your father,' she continued. 'I do hope . . . oh, my God, you must excuse me.' She stood up, put a hand on her stomach and staggered away. Presumably things were not quite right with the artificial workings of her body.

For just a short while I felt she had been able to forget the awful contraption which was attached to her, but then nature had taken over in the cruellest of forms, pulling her back to the present, to the 1960s, to a time of colostomies,

when the victims did not always recuperate in the homes
of their less than helpful daughters, when the rest of Britain
was swinging, when, according to Mr Macmillan, we had
never had it so good.

But was it so good? I simply recall it as an era when my
mother was suffering, when George and I were having
unexpected difficulties, when Adam became withdrawn
and I began wondering what life was all about.

True, it wouldn't have been possible for my mother to
convalesce at Ackerley – at least, in the initial stages – as
she needed professional attention. But I was sorry that
George had 'shown his colours', as it were. With regard
to the future, I simply dared not look ahead, at any rate,
not until my mother had seen Mr Steiner again.

She was taken in an ambulance back to the London
hospital for an appointment with him one raw November
day. I arranged to meet them both there and, while my
mother was being escorted back to the ambulance, he had
a private word with me.

'I'm afraid . . . the situation is irreversible.'

'I see.' I think I had known that would be the verdict.
Then something made me add, 'Is she . . . it . . . likely to
get worse?'

'It's always possible.'

'What do you suggest . . . I mean, about future care?'

'I think she should stay where she is for at least another
month. Get perfectly used to managing her new apparatus.
Some people adapt more quickly than others. Your mother
is a fastidious woman. It doesn't come easily to her. How
big is her flat? Could you get her some living-in help? I
don't necessarily mean a nurse.'

He had tactfully made no suggestion that she should
come to me. All the same, I coloured.

'It's small, but there is a second bedroom.'

'Good. I think that might be your best bet. Why don't
you advertise in *The Lady*? By the time she leaves The
Laurels, I think she would simply need a sympathetic
companion, but of course it would be a help if such a
person had a little knowledge of nursing.'

During that winter I seemed to live with *The Lady*. I

advertised regularly, because no sooner had I engaged one person than within a short space of time – sometimes even days – clashes would occur and I would have to find someone else. To say that my mother was difficult was a gross understatement. Having been so tough and energetic all her life – indeed, I couldn't remember her ever being laid low – she just wasn't able to come to terms with such a devastating illness. It seemed as if her whole character altered. She also became extremely worried about money. She resented both having to have help and the thought of anyone else paying for it. Yet she knew the only alternative – except, of course, it wasn't an alternative because of George's attitude, although naturally she was unaware of this – was to come to Ackerley. But seeing that hitherto she would never stop a night with us, I do not know whether she seriously considered the idea although, as one companion after another departed, she could well have thought it the lesser of two evils.

When she first returned home at the beginning of December, I had engaged a Miss Fisk, who was said to be quiet, honest and used to dealing with old people. She was fifty and, at interview, seemed pleasant enough. When I took her to The Laurels to see my mother, the meeting had not gone off too badly. It was agreed that she would settle in at Chiswick two days before my mother came out of the nursing-home, in order to get the place ready for her.

Within a week, the complaints began. My mother telephoned me early one morning and asked me to come at once.

'Are you feeling ill?'

'No. No more than usual, that is.'

I drove to Chiswick, parked the car in the quiet road outside her flat and saw, from the twitch of the curtains – she lived on the ground floor – that my mother had been watching out for me.

Once in her sitting-room with the door closed, she came straight to the point.

'Miss Fisk will be leaving on Friday.'

'On *Friday*?'

'Yes. She drinks.'

'But Mother how . . . what makes you think so?'

'The sherry decanter was over half full on my arrival. I actually offered her a glass that evening. Very silly of me. One should never start that sort of thing. She has obviously been at it ever since.'

I took a look at the offending decanter. It was still over a quarter full. Even if Miss Fisk *had* helped herself to a glass or two, I could hardly blame her. Cooped up with my mother all day, she probably needed some fortification. Besides, Mother might well have had a little tipple herself. It was the one drink she occasionally indulged in.

'Did you accuse Miss Fisk of this?' I asked her.

'Yes.'

'And what did she say?'

'She flatly denied it. She reminded me that the Reverend Mr Milner had called the morning before last and she had asked him to help himself because I wasn't quite ready to receive him.'

'*Well*, then. That answers it.'

'Mr Milner would never have had more than one.'

I tried to visualise Mr Milner. We had met once, soon after my mother had moved in. He was a pale, nervous man, who looked as if he could well do with some sort of boost to his morale now and then, rather like Miss Fisk.

'Mother, are you sure *you* haven't had a glass or two?'

'Quite sure. I had a small one the first evening with Miss Fisk, but it didn't agree with me.'

'Well, it all seems a storm in a teacup. Just badly mismanaged. I'll go and see Miss Fisk.'

'There's really no point, Vicky. Neither of us is likely to change our minds.'

All the same, I went into the kitchen, where I found the poor woman making a shepherd's pie. To my consternation and amazement, she was red from the neck up, just as Great-Granny Alice had described Miss James. My mother's companion gave every indication that she, too, was going through the Change.

'Miss Fisk,' I said, 'I am so sorry to hear about what has happened between you and my mother. I'm sure it's all a terrible mistake.'

She looked at me out of reproachful watery blue eyes and then turned to the stove to stir something in a saucepan.

'Once confidence has been lost,' she said, in a muffled kind of way, 'it can seldom be rekindled, Mrs Norbury. I shall be leaving on Friday.'

'But . . .' I thought of Christmas, only eighteen shopping days away, as the announcer on the radio had gleefully reminded us that morning. I couldn't get a stopgap at such short notice, could I? Mother would have to come to us. George couldn't refuse at Christmastime. Or could he? He was showing a side of his character that I had never known existed, rather as Mother was doing. I felt bewildered, miserable and angry with everyone, especially myself. Why couldn't I cope? Why was I not more like Great-Granny Alice?

'Miss Fisk,' I went on. 'If I convince my mother that she has been mistaken, couldn't you . . . ?'

She turned back and faced me. 'I'm sorry, Mrs Norbury. In any case, I should have been giving in my notice in the New Year. The post is not to my liking.'

So that was that.

Friday, I said to myself, as I left. You have three days. Three days in which to find someone who will cope with an irascible, colostomised old lady. Why, the archangel Gabriel wouldn't take it on.

I drove into central London to call at some agencies, as I had told my mother I would do. I don't know how much she realised how desperate the situation was, how difficult she was making things for me, how much she resented the fact that I hadn't immediately invited her to Ackerley, even if she refused to come. Or whether she really thought she would be all right on her own, as she intimated. To me, in those days, she simply wasn't the mother I had known, any more than George was the same husband.

The woman at the agency was young and sophisticated. I felt she could easily have been an ex-debutante. Not that she wasn't sympathetic. Her big brown mascaraed eyes looked at me with what seemed genuine concern. Except that I knew her age made it impossible for her really to understand the situation. You have to live through a thing of this kind to know what it's like. She appeared to have no one on her books at the moment who would be the slightest use to me. But she did come up with one unexpectedly helpful suggestion.

'What about Universal Aunts? Have you tried them? They can't give permanent service but they do help people out of a hole for around three weeks.'

'Really? It's an idea. Thank you very much. Meanwhile, would you let me know if anyone suitable comes along?'

'Of course.' She smiled sweetly, stood up and ushered me out. Nice girl, I thought, as I went down the stairs. I believed she would honestly keep trying on my behalf.

While I was about it, I went to two more agencies and put my name down. One of them told me of a widow called Mrs Kimberley, but she came from Aberdeen which was a drawback from the interviewing aspect. Besides, why did she want to come so far south?

Tired, deflated and worried sick, I went home and rang Universal Aunts.

6

By a sheer stroke of luck, I got an 'Aunt' for Christmas. She was a hard-up widow, whose husband had died the previous December. She wanted temporary work over the festive season and, because of the associations of a year ago, one where there would be no festivities. In the New Year, she was emigrating to live with her brother and his wife in South Africa. Her name was Mrs Everton and she seemed a kindly, sensible body. She was certainly the only help during that ghastly time whom my mother took to; and, in a curious way, I believe she quite took to my mother. The fact that Mrs Everton was off to Cape Town on January 3rd was a great blow, possibly to the three of us, because I believe for two pins she might have been persuaded to remain on a permanent basis. Yet, looking at the situation logically – which I am sure Mrs Everton did – it was extremely doubtful how permanent a job of this sort could be. Somehow, I did not think my mother would be with us next Christmas.

Nor was she.

A Mrs Bancroft followed Mrs Everton. A Miss Fulford followed Mrs Bancroft. A Mrs Maloney followed Miss Fulford. And all the while I watched my mother failing – as Great-Granny Alice might have said – as well as becoming more cantankerous.

As the weeks and months passed, I tried to spend as much time with her as I could. I like to think my visits were of some comfort. Often, I felt she wanted to tell me something and then changed her mind, but certainly whenever we got on to Great-Granny Alice and her diaries, she always seemed to rally a little and become more expansive.

'Adam will be very glad one day, Vicky, that you're doing what you're doing. He'll be able to show his own children a book about his ancestors.'

She seemed convinced that there *would* be a book published. I hadn't the heart to put doubts into her mind, although there were plenty in mine. For one thing, I was a novice and by no means certain I was going about the task in the right way: marking the passages I wanted typed, making explanatory notes where necessary, writing short linking passages to give coherence to the whole – or so I hoped. It was taking a long time, a commodity which seemed in increasingly short supply. There were my almost daily visits to Chiswick, transporting Adam to and from school – although George sometimes helped out over this – arranging for the child to be cared for whenever I was out, although he was now thankfully at an age when he was much more self-sufficient, and the constant wearying business of advertising, contacting agencies, interviewing and organising the arrival and departure of my mother's string of unsatisfactory companions.

But there was no doubt that Great-Granny Alice helped me over that period, as she did my mother. Just thinking about her and finding a few moments to read her beautiful script was somehow therapeutic, even though I knew I fell so very far short of her high ideals.

It must have been about June when we got on to discussing Alice's death. I had been wanting to ask my mother about it but, in view of her own condition, I hadn't liked to. Yet I felt it was important for me to know because, so far as I could judge, Great-Granny Alice had not written much after 1888, when she appeared to be ill. I had not had time to make any detailed foray into that period as yet, but taking a quick look through her entries towards the end of her life there were discreet references to an indisposition which she was obviously averse to describing. Certainly, her diaries were not then kept with the same regularity or attention to detail, although her innate stoicism was ever apparent. I badly wanted to know exactly what had ailed her.

Fortunately and quite unexpectedly, my mother remarked one day, 'You know, Vicky, I think Great-Granny Alice had what I've got. I mean, without the operation.'

'What makes you say that?'

'Well, Hannah once told me that, before she died, her mother used to spend a lot of time on her commode. Even in a house such as Ivers, sanitation was still pretty primitive

in those days. There were commodes and chamber-pots
for use indoors and then a large outside earth closet with
several holes cut in its long wooden seat. Hannah said that
Dr Allingham, who was getting to be an old man, would
drive up from the village in his pony and trap most days
to see her mother and that he kept prescribing purgatives.
I suppose Alice had a stoppage. Hannah also said that, on
looking back, she realised her mother must have suffered
a lot of pain but, being the kind of person she was, she
kept her troubles to herself. Cancer was never mentioned,
but Hannah's sisters often referred to the fact that their
mother had had an early Change, just as Dr Allingham
had predicted. They seem to have connected this in their
minds with her final illness and even went as far as to hint
that it was all Lionel's fault for not showing more restraint
after each birth. There seems to have been a lot of muddled
thinking on their part, but young girls in those days were
kept very much in the dark about all that kind of thing.
Anyway, on Alice's death certificate Dr Allingham simply
wrote *Ulcerative Colitis*. No wonder, with all the senna she
kept taking.'

'I see. And Lionel? What happened to him?'

'Oh, he was devastated by Alice's death. He had no
idea how ill she was. He lived a little longer and was
looked after by his two unmarried daughters, your great-
aunts, Phoebe and Fanny. Then he suddenly got a car-
buncle on his neck and was gone in the matter of days.
Septicaemia set in. There were no antibiotics to save him
then.'

'I see,' I said again. While we were on the subject, I
hoped I wasn't being unfeeling in pursuing the causes of
death a little further. 'And my grandparents, whom I
never knew? You've never told me much about what
happened, other than it was a motoring accident.'

'Yes, well that was very sad. It was just after the First
World War. My father had bought a Hispano-Suiza. He'd
done very well for himself as a merchant banker. We had
this big house in Hampstead and he'd go off to the City
each day in his top hat and spats. On Sunday afternoons
he would take my mother out for a "spin", as he used to

call it. She loved that. He was very proud of his car but
even more proud of her. She was getting on for fifty, but
she was still very pretty and she always dressed beautifully. She had special motoring outfits made, not quite the
ones with those big hats and veils women wore before
the war, but she had a marvellous tussore dust-coat for
summer and a West of England cloth coat for winter with
a huge fur collar and a fur muff. It was all rather touching,
as she still used to lean forward going uphill and backwards
on going down, just as she was taught to do in the pony-
trap when she was a girl. Sometimes I would go with
them, but on this fated occasion, I was away teaching.
They'd gone to their favourite spot, Box Hill, which was
quite a jaunt in those days. No one really knew what
happened for the car was completely smashed up but,
according to some picnickers on the hillside, it just seemed
to career out of control. I suppose the brakes failed. I
remember being sent for, along with my brother and sister.
It was a terrible time . . .'

My mother's voice trailed away. It was obvious she had
been very fond of her parents and, that afternoon, had
given me another clue as to why she had married my father
so soon after their death. But I felt it was now definitely
time to talk of other things.

'I hope,' I said, 'that you'll change your mind about
coming down to Maplethorpe in August with Adam and
me. We could give Mrs Maloney a little break and she
could join us later.'

My mother frowned. 'You mean a *holiday* for Mrs M?
She's only been here six weeks. I've already told you. I
shall do no such thing.'

'But . . . Mother. Just think, I won't be able to visit you
like I'm doing now. I shan't feel happy being away so
long.'

'Well, if you must bury yourself in the back of beyond,
that's your business. Personally, I can't see why you want
to continue going there. No doubt the place served its
purpose after Adam's illness, but that seems no good
reason for making staying there an annual event.'

'But Adam loves it, Mother. He's made such friends

with the children at the nearby farm. He's been looking forward to it all the year.'

I had been looking forward to it as well, although to a lesser degree. For, if I were honest with myself, the thought of my mother and Mrs Maloney accompanying us took away a lot of the enjoyable anticipation. I felt both relieved yet guilty at my mother's firm stand.

'No,' she said, 'we've discussed this before, Vicky, and it's out of the question.' Then, to my surprise, she continued, 'You talk about your concern at leaving me. But have you not thought that it is rather a long time to leave your husband?'

She had never before made such a direct reference to my marriage. One of her many good points was that she did not interfere, although I sometimes wondered what she was thinking.

'George doesn't mind,' I answered quickly. 'It's difficult for him to get away in the summer. And, of course, living over a club, it's not as if he isn't *catered* for, if you see what I mean.'

She looked away. 'Men need more than mere catering for, Vicky.'

I stared at her. My mother. Trying to give me some sort of sex advice at this late stage in our lives? I thought of her and my father, and how they had always seemed like a friendly brother and sister. I thought of my Grandmother Hannah and her husband who, from all I had heard of them, would appear to have been much more like man and wife. I thought of Alice and Lionel, begetting five children and how those children felt that Lionel should have shown more restraint. I wondered whether Lionel had refrained from sexual intercourse after Dr Allingham's warnings about further pregnancies. Or had he then *strayed*? Or had the early Change, to which Alice often referred, been nature's way of conveniently allowing him to sleep with his wife again? If so, what would Alice's reaction have been? The diaries would never tell me that, any more than my mother would ever tell me how it was between her and my father. Perhaps all children get it wrong about that side of their parents' relationship. It is always rather putting off to think of them engaged in such an undignified and unparental exercise.

But had my mother, with a wisdom born of age and experience, pointed out something in my own marriage to which I had turned a blind eye and refused to face? There flashed through my mind the old adage: *When my eyes close, yours will open*.

Perhaps George *did* want more than mere catering. We hadn't slept together for quite a while, a state of affairs which I thought had come about by unspoken mutual agreement. I had not missed having sex. In fact, it was a relief. I had imagined George felt the same. He seemed to me, especially as he got older, to derive his pleasures from eating and drinking – he had put on an enormous amount of weight – from being hail-fellow-well-met at the club, from being 'one of the boys' and being called 'Colonel' by all and sundry. Although he was invariably engaged in conversation, I had never actually noticed him chat up a female. He might have been a bit of a lady-killer in his younger wartime days – after all, incredible as it now seems, there had been a strong physical attraction between us, which is why we married, saving me, just, from what was then considered a fate worse than death – but afterwards he had never given me cause to think he had been, or even would like to have been, unfaithful.

But it could be that I was wrong. Perhaps if I had been a more satisfactory wife in every sense of the word, he would never have behaved in the way he had about not having my mother to Ackerley for her convalescence.

And then came a last most unwelcome thought: had my mother always refused to stay with us because she sensed something was wrong and did not want to make it worse? Did she know a great deal more than she ever let on? In fact, did Mother know best?

I came away that day feeling curiously small and insignificant.

Three weeks before Adam and I were due to go to Maplethorpe and the day before I had arranged for her solicitor to call because she had announced she wished to make a codicil to her will, my mother suddenly died.

7

Mamma died ten days ago. Very peacefully, in her sleep. She had only been at Ivers six months, but I shall always be glad to think she was living with us at the end. Since Christmas, her mental state seemed to deteriorate daily. It was often as if she did not know any of us, except Miss Clutterbuck. It was fortunate that Lionel suggested Mamma make a new Will last autumn when she was more in possession of her faculties. I am delighted that she left Miss C. thirty-five pounds. The poor woman is quite overcome.

The rest of Mamma's Estate is divided between the girls. I am to have her jewellery which, of course, I shall pass on to them. I trust there will be no lasting ill-feeling because she did not remember her other children, but I know how strongly she disapproved of Harry's gambling and she felt my sisters could have visited her more frequently. I did my best to explain they all lived over twenty miles away. At the funeral I fear they were somewhat contrary. Agatha seemed to imply that I had been currying favour by accommodating Mamma. Such a thought would never have crossed my mind.

The Reverend Mr Graham conducted the Service splendidly. It was well attended. The Earl and Countess of Dewhurst honoured us with their presence. All the flowers were really beautiful, the more so it seemed, being winter-time. The Dewhurst wreath was white carnations and chrysanthemums from their own hot-houses, on which Lady Dewhurst had written in her own hand: 'With our deepest sympathy.' They sat immediately behind us in the church.

I have packed up Mamma's clothes for Charity. She always had an eye for a good piece of material. There were several lengths of West of England cloth, as well as some hanks of wool. I propose to give one or two to Widow Shergold. Percy continues to give good service and Lionel has put him in the dairy, as the herd is to be increased, cows being now more profitable than corn-growing.

Rather to my surprise, George proved to be the greatest assistance over my mother's funeral. One might have thought he had been burying people all his life. He seemed to know all about obtaining death certificates and dealing with lawyers and funeral directors. I tried to stifle the thought that his helpfulness and our sudden easier relationship was due to relief on both our parts that my mother had died.

He and I, in a funeral car, followed the hearse bearing her coffin to Golders Green Crematorium on a horribly bright summer morning, where the Reverend Mr Milner conducted the short service nervously but, I suppose, adequately. I'm afraid I was unable to stop thinking about him helping himself to my mother's sherry, and wishing that there had been someone more like the Reverend Mr Graham taking care of things *and* that we were having a family burial in a village church like Great-Granny Alice's Mamma had been given.

Only a handful of people turned up: three of my mother's old friends, who had read the notices George had put in *The Times* and the *Telegraph*, Mrs Maloney, the steward from the club and two couples who were members, an old school friend of mine, Jill Patterson, and another who was with me in the ATS, both of whom lived in London. I realised how lonely and desolate my mother's existence had become since my father's death, how she had never really settled in Chiswick and the new life I had hoped she might make had never materialised. She had been too old to uproot. It might have been better to have found her some small place near Canterbury amongst people she had known, however difficult it might have been for me to care for her at such a distance, especially during her last illness.

As I watched her coffin slide away into that ghastly yawning point of no return, I thought about after-life and wished devoutly I could believe in it. But I couldn't. And yet . . . it seemed strange that Alice was still very much with me. She was so *real* in my mind. I could picture Ivers and her and Lionel and the children and the outside closet, with all the holes. Did they *really* have that kind of communal arrangement for such a private and personal function? I supposed it was a most sensible precaution for a big family, especially when one of its members got caught short.

I knew that such thoughts were almost sacrilegious on such an occasion, yet they supported me. I felt that because of Alice, I, Mrs Victoria Norbury, wife of George, mother of Adam, had been given being. I was a descendant of fine farming stock and had a great-grandmother who thought more about other people than she did about herself. What a lesson. There was no Widow Shergold in my own life, no Percy and my own mother had never been under my roof at the end. I did not even collect jumble for any local fête. I was flotsam compared to Alice.

George had laid in a certain amount of drink at my mother's flat, in case anyone might care to come back there after the service. I extended such an invitation as we stood around, rather awkwardly, outside the Crematorium. Mr Milner thanked me effusively, but regretted that other commitments prevented him from accepting. The steward and one of the couples from the club made further excuses. Two of my mother's old friends said they had to get home and I arranged for them to have a lift back into central London with the couple who were returning to Surrey. In the end, only the other couple, one of my mother's friends, Jill Patterson and Mrs Maloney came back to Chiswick, to drink sherry or spirits and nibble at the sandwiches which the latter had prepared earlier that morning.

Is this, I wondered, as I handed round refreshments, what happened to so many lives at the end? When someone or other is of no more use, only a liability, has outlived his or her time – or, at any rate, *useful* time – when sibling, child, in-law or some more distant relative or friend, has to attend to this departure business, inescapably being forced into form-filling, decisions regarding types of coffins, dates and times about the disposal of that coffin together with its contents, and the question of a stone or a rose bush or a name in a book, as a token of remembrance.

And how long were the dead *really* remembered? Great men and women went down in history books, but how much and in what way were they remembered by their nearest and dearest? I hoped I would long remember my mother. I was sure I would remember – or rather, treasure – my newly-found knowledge of Great-Granny Alice. I resolved that when I came back from Maplethorpe that year I would visit her grave. Adam would be at boarding-school and I would have much more time to myself.

I drove him down to Pennyford on August 1st, as planned, together with the greater part of his uniform which I had somehow managed to buy and which now needed marking. I had sorted out and packed up some of my mother's goods and chattels which had been left to me. I felt the rest could safely wait until my return, when I would put her flat on the market. She had also left me two thousand pounds outright, but the bulk of her Estate was to go, in trust, for Adam. I was glad about this, for he and she had always had a special relationship and, on the occasions when I had taken him to see her during her last illness, he had seemed even more subdued and withdrawn after-wards. I hoped a holiday at Maplethorpe would help him. The thing which distressed me was not knowing what my mother had wanted to put in the codicil she was unable to make, so that I could have carried out her wishes.

I asked George if he would care to join Adam and me, at any rate for a weekend or two, and this he agreed to do. In some strange way, I think the three of us were closer at that time or, at least, in more accord, than we had been for a long while.

The Colberts were, as ever, extremely kind and, on the Saturday of George's first visit, Edward gave him a pleasant hour or so driving him round Warreners in his Land Rover. One of my husband's greatest assets has always been his knack of spontaneously getting on with all and sundry, even if only on a superficial level and he had little in common with them. I suppose the adjutant and club-man in him invariably came to the fore.

That evening, as I sat sewing name-tapes on some of Adam's uniform, I began to feel that George was really enjoying Maplethorpe but then, suddenly, it simply wasn't enough for him. On the Sunday, Edward was worried

because a field of barley had gone down badly in a thunder-
storm the previous night and the mechanics were still
unable to trace a fault in his one and only combine. I could
sense George becoming restless. He had never been much
of a reader, disliked walking and loathed gardening, even
though he had a good knowledge of putting-greens and
how to look after them. The weather that day precluded a
trip to the beach and there was a limit to how much
television even George could watch.

'I think I'll be getting back, old girl,' he said, after lunch.
'We've got this tournament coming up on Tuesday. I'd
like to see everything's in order. I'll be down again in a
fortnight.'

I waved him goodbye – Adam was playing with the
Colbert children – and returned to the house. It looked like
more rain, so I sat down indoors to work on Great-Granny
Alice's diaries, with August 1876 very much to the fore.
Amongst other references to harvest and the weather –
which seemed to have been uncommonly like today's –
she had written, *The most amazing man called Alexander Bell
has invented a Contraption whereby people can speak to each other
at a distance by means of Wires. One can scarcely believe it. It is
said that our beloved Queen is most impressed – as well as Mr
Disraeli.*

I sat there in front of the little desk in the drawing-room
at Maplethorpe, her diary almost touching the telephone.
I had only to lift Alice's *Contraption* to speak to almost
anyone in the world. Yet the only person I should like to
have spoken to at that moment was Great-Granny Alice.
All I could do was to stare at her copperplate handwriting
and the faded sepia photograph I kept by me. There she
was, immaculately coiffured, sitting perfectly erect, her
fine direct eyes staring back at me with a mixture of
benevolence, wisdom, pride and, yes, something more.
Fearlessness, perhaps, or was it faith? She seemed a person
at peace with herself. I knew she would never be one to
need the tranquillisers which present-day doctors kept
prescribing. Even my own GP had enquired whether I
would like some Librium to help me over my mother's last
illness.

I wondered what Alice's family had been doing on the day she wrote about that embryonic telephone. Hannah, my grandmother, would have been about four or five. As it was August and the weather 'caddling' – as they still describe tricky weather in the west country – was Lionel being difficult? Were his men able to carry on scything and stooking? Possibly. At least they wouldn't have been held up by a combine breaking down. So long as it was not a Sunday, twenty or thirty farm hands would have been out there and at it, just as soon as the sun shone, instead of the two or three frustrated individuals I knew were now up in Long Croft, gnashing their teeth as they fiddled with an immobilised combine. But in a changing world, it gave me a great sense of stability and continuity to know that, however many contraptions were brought into being, the corn would still be gathered in somehow. There was still seed-time and harvest, *a time to plant*, as *Ecclesiastes* said, *and a time to pluck up that which is planted . . . a time to be born and a time to die*.

Great-Granny Alice's time to die was some way off yet, thank God. I still had plenty more diaries to go through. She wasn't to know what was in store for her at the end, any more than my mother knew. And I, at the age of forty-three, had scarcely given a thought to my own de-mise. I had made a Will, of course, but, barring accidents, my death seemed a long way off. I was at the stage of life when I was looking forward to my son's possible achievements at school, at college, at his chosen occupation and, later on, to seeing him married. I supposed that one day he would have children, but I simply could not envisage becoming a grandmother. That was much too far ahead to think about.

I was still young. I still had so much to learn.

8

In Treasured Memory
of
Alice Mabel Louise
Medway
Born 1839 – Died 1889
Beloved Wife
of
Lionel Francis Medway
Blessed Are The Pure In Heart
The Will of The Lord Be Done

I stood by Alice's grave while the autumn sunlight played
on the lichen-covered headstone. I had had to do a little
scraping with a latch-key in order to read the full inscrip-
tion. I was glad to find that her character had been so
fittingly acknowledged. Would it have been Lionel or his
daughters who had thought of the wording of the epitaph?

Next to it lay Lionel's own headstone. This was inscribed
in what seemed to be a rather more naïve, almost jocular
fashion:

Behold the Husband and the Wife
Now joined in Death as once in Life.
We trust the change is for the Best
To live with Christ and be at Rest.

Who was responsible for choosing that little verse, I wondered. Could it have been Hannah, my grandmother? She
would have been at an age when that kind of verse might
have appealed to her.

It was very peaceful in the churchyard. I straightened
up and looked around me. The beech trees behind the wall
on the south side had turned golden, the elm by the
lych-gate showed lemon patches. There were spindle ber-
ries in the hedgerow leading up to it. Not many graves
bore witness to new inhabitants. Presumably some other
burial ground had had to be found. Perhaps not only

convenience but lack of space made people nowadays ask to be cremated – as well, of course, as not having the same kind of feelings about the sanctity of a human corpse.

It occurred to me that I might even discover my great-great-grandmother's grave and this, in due course, I did, but not before I had come across a very small stone by which something – I know not what – made me pause. I leant down and, almost before I started to scratch at the lichen, I knew what I would find: *Percival John Shergold 1863-1933*. Dear Percy. He had had a good innings for those days. Just to think, he had been still alive when I had reached my teens. I could have met him, talked to him, asked him about Ivers, what it was like working for Lionel. But then, sadly, I realised that I wouldn't have been bothered. What young girl of thirteen wants to ask some old-age-pensioner about his past as a farm labourer? Indeed, even when I was a lot older I still hadn't been the slightest bit interested in editing Alice's diaries.

What *was* it about advancing years that made a person hark back to the past? Was it a craving to know more about where he or she came from because the present wasn't all that good? Or simply a nostalgia for a time one was *certain* was better, when summers were hotter, when life was calmer, sweeter, kinder. Yet, was it, really? Perhaps, but only for some. I tried to think back to the early thirties. Percy would have died during the depression. I remembered how worried my father then was. There were hunger marches. Jarrow seemed to come to mind. Percy seemed to have begun and ended his life in bad times. He had been sent into the dairy at the age of ten or eleven because cheap wheat was flooding the market and Lionel found cows brought a better return. Much the same was happening when Percy had been laid to rest in this churchyard. I wondered whether he had ever mastered one of those old Ford tractors which I recalled arriving at the nurseries with a trailer of manure behind it. I was glad to find that he had married, although that was only to be expected. His wife, Agnes Miriam, lay beside him. There must have been something rather comforting in those days for a married couple to know that they would eventually end up side by side, joined in death, as the epitaph ran on Lionel's grave, as they were in life.

There was a small noise behind me and I turned to see a very young parson leaning his bicycle against the lych-gate. He came towards me, smiling. He looked as if he could still only have been in his early twenties.

'Good morning. Were you just looking round? It's a pleasant church and churchyard, isn't it?' He was obviously very pleased to find someone taking an interest in his little domain.

'Yes,' I answered. 'At least, I haven't been inside the church yet. I was looking for the graves of my ancestors.'

'Really? I hope you found them.'

'Yes. My great-grandparents, actually. They both died in this village round about the 1890s. The name was Medway. My great-grandfather farmed Ivers farm.'

The young man before me looked puzzled. 'Ivers farm? I don't think. . . . Oh, I see. Yes, of course. There's a house called Ivers in the village but the farm has been amalgamated with a whole lot of others. A company from London bought them all up. I'm afraid we suffer from the barley-baron epidemic here. An airline pilot, an Australian, lives at Ivers, although he's not often at home, as you can imagine. Name of Tanner. His wife and he have three small children. Pleasant people.'

'Really?'

I had a sudden fierce overwhelming desire to see Ivers. 'Do you think,' I asked, 'Mrs Tanner would mind if I called?'

'Prue? Good heavens, no. She's a honey.'

I looked at him. Almost, I laughed. He really seemed so *very* young. But nice. I couldn't imagine the Reverend Mr Graham, who had conducted Alice's funeral, ever referring to one of his parishioners as a 'honey', even if the expression had been coined in those days. For that matter, I couldn't think of nervous Mr Milner doing so either. There was something most refreshing about this boyish enthusiastic cleric standing before me, bicycle clips round his trousers, his long fair hair blowing in the wind.

'If you like,' he continued, 'I'll come up to Ivers with

you and introduce you to Prue. My name's Alaric Reed, by the way. I just want to unlock the vestry so that the cleaner can get in. It's awful these days the way we have to take such precautions. I'm in charge of three parishes and they're all the same. Vandalism right the way down the valley. There's a kind of nucleus of bad boys round here and somehow I want to get at them, fire them with some sort of community spirit. I think I may be winning. Next Sunday we're going to have a service here and sing a few of the Beatles' songs at the end. I thought that might at least get them into the church. Once I can do that, I would be half-way there, don't you think?'

'Er . . . yes,' I replied, rather lamely, as we walked towards the church together. Surely Alice and Lionel and Mamma would start turning in their graves if *She Loves Me, Yeah, Yeah, Yeah* came belting out into the churchyard.

I wandered round inside the church while he went into the vestry, saw the pew which I imagined might have belonged to the Medway family, imagined them in the very front row at Mamma's funeral, with Lord and Lady Dewhurst immediately behind, looked up at the pulpit where the Reverend Mr Graham would have given probably an inspired address. I noted the flowers on the altar and thought of those other ones which Alice had written about: the wreath of white carnations and chrysanthemums from the Dewhurst hot-houses. And I knelt down, just briefly, and sent up a little prayer. God knows what or why, but it seemed the thing to do and I was strangely moved.

When the young rector or vicar or whatever he was called came out of the vestry, he said, 'I like this church best of the ones I look after. We only have a service every third Sunday, which is sad.'

We walked towards the door and I found myself asking, 'What made you go into the Ministry?'

He waited until we were outside again before replying, 'Hard to say, really. I was up at Oxford reading P.P.E. and suddenly I thought it would be a good thing to do. I felt there must be something *more* than just this philosophy stuff, something no one truly understood but which made them better people for trying. I expect I'm expressing this very badly, but I just knew that that's what I wanted to do. I suppose you'd say I had a call. Are you a believer?'

I hesitated. I didn't think I was and yet, I had sent up a short prayer only minutes ago. Why? Was it superstition, hope, a safeguard just in case . . . ?

'I'm not an atheist or an agnostic,' I said, at length. 'I'd like to think there is something else, but it's difficult.'

'Bloody difficult. I know just what you mean.'

We walked through the village, Alaric pushing his bicycle. He really was delightfully human. I hoped he would have success with his bad boys. He deserved to.

'That's Ivers,' he said, suddenly, pointing up a lane to where a long low stone house, roofed by old tiles, lay flanked on either side by two giant oaks.

So this was where Great-Granny Alice had lived and died. I could hardly wait to get inside.

Prue Tanner came to the door wearing jeans and a faded shirt, her golden hair framing a pale oval face out of which two enormous blue eyes regarded us with interest. At her side a small girl, aged about three and a complete replica of her mother, also gazed at us, but suspiciously. I could quite see why my new parson friend had described Prue as a 'honey'.

Having introduced me and explained the reason for our call, he left me in her welcoming hands and cycled away. She took me with pleasure and pride into every room, telling me along the way all about the changes she and her husband had made, how ten years ago Ivers had still been a farmhouse, how they had knocked down walls to create more feeling of space, put in a second bathroom and a downstairs cloakroom. I simply had to tell her then about the outside privy with all the holes.

She laughed out loud. 'I expect that must have been where we've made a utility room. I keep my deep freeze and washing-machine in it. Dear God. Just think. How on earth did they cope with dirty laundry in those days? All those nappies.'

'Yes,' I replied. 'But apparently there was a Widow Shergold who did some of it, even though my great-grandmother had maids. This poor widow had a little boy called Percy who used to trundle the clean and dirty to and fro in a wheelbarrow. He started work at Ivers farm as a bird-scarer at the age of ten for a shilling a week.'

Prue was silent for a while. Then she said, 'Perhaps we haven't progressed all that much after all. I mean, I've no maids and I've got all these gadgets, but there's only one pair of hands to work them. Mine. I don't seem to have any spare time. It'll be easier when this little person goes to nursery school.' She ruffled the hair of her youngest child – who I had been told was called Caroline – affectionately. 'I suppose your great-grandmother had nursemaids as well.'

'Yes.'

'I bet they were a lot happier than some of the au pairs and mother's helps one comes across round here. All that most of them want to do is to get off every night on the bus to the nearest town. They're often more trouble than they're worth. I'm without one at the moment. That reminds me. I shall have to go soon to pick up my middle daughter. She has morning lessons in the next village. We've just time for a cup of coffee. Then, if you like, I could drop you somewhere.'

'It's kind of you,' I said, 'but I've got my car. Down by the church. But I'd love some coffee if it's not too much trouble.'

We sat drinking it in Prue's ultra-modern kitchen at a kind of bar where the family evidently took most of their meals. I looked out of the window at the view of the downs, with their little clumps of trees on top just like gold and green pincushions, and thought of Great-Granny Alice doing the same. Then I remembered. She would never have done anything of the sort. She would never have sat down drinking and gossiping in her kitchen. Her maids would have done that. Or would they? Hardly. Such behaviour would have been deemed justification for dismissal. Although I suspected Alice was a kinder and fairer mistress than most, I had read one entry in her diary which referred to having to stop a housemaid's one half-day a month because she had neglected to dust along the top of the pictures in the dining-room.

Perhaps the present time *was* better – at least for some – after all.

9

I came back to Ackerley having promised Prue Tanner that I would make another visit. She had even offered to put me up at Ivers and I must say I couldn't help thinking it would be rather enjoyable to sleep under Great-Granny Alice's roof. There were also several other things I wanted to do when I had more time, such as going through the parish records and making enquiries as to whether some of the Shergold descendants were still living in the district. But, for the moment, I was anxious to get home, as I had left long before the post arrived that day and I was hoping to hear from Adam. Although our holiday at Maplethorpe had certainly done the child good, I knew that because of his feelings for his maternal grandmother, the ordeal of going away to boarding-school had come at an unfortunate time.

There was, indeed, a letter addressed to George and myself in Adam's rather well-formed script, as well as another for me alone in a hand I did not recognise. George had kindly refrained from opening our son's so that we might do so together. Eagerly, I slit the envelope and began to read out loud:

Dear Mummy and Daddy,

So far, so good. It isn't as bad here as I thought it might be. No one has said much about my not playing rugger etc. Believe it or not, there is another chap in my dormitory who's excused also, anyway, for the time being. He is bronkitick. His name is Julian Wainwright. Could we take him out when you come down one Sunday? His father is abroad and his mother lives miles away in Yorkshire. The food is passabel. The housemaster and his wife are nice.

I hope you will be able to sort out all Gran's things and sell her flat. Until that's done I don't suppose there is much time for the diaries.

Could you please send that big old navy swetter I always wore at Maplethorpe. It would be usefull for outdoor 'projects' at weekends. Julian and I are planning to make a large-scale

model village. Also have you got those last photos of Maple-
thorpe developed? The ones with Herbie and the Colberts
combine in?

    Hope you're both well,

                        Love,
                        Adam.

'He's *all right*,' said George. 'Boarding-school's just what
he needed. Being among boys of his own age all the
time. And I dare say it'll even improve his spelling in due
course.'

With relief, I could only agree. After George had gone
back down to the club for a last look round – for it had
been late when I returned – I almost forgot to open the
other letter, as I was thinking so hard about Adam and
how surprisingly quickly he seemed to have settled down.
Eventually, I picked it up and opened it, expecting I knew
not what, possibly something to do with my mother or
even a bill.

It did, indeed, indirectly have something to do with her,
but nothing I could possibly have bargained for. *Dear Mrs
Norbury,* I read. *I have been wondering whether or not to
approach you since happening to see the notice of your mother's
death in the newspaper at the beginning of July. Please would
you accept my belated sympathy. She was a good person and very
kind to me.*

Puzzled, I read on,

> *I find it difficult to tell you the real reason for this letter, as it
> would be easier if we could meet. Is there any chance that you
> would be prepared to do this? As you can see from the address,
> I live in Southampton, but I would come up to London at any
> time convenient to you.*
>
> *I am sorry if this sounds mysterious but, as I have said,
> it isn't easy to put my reasons on paper. I hope you will
> understand.*

                Yours sincerely,
                Janet Palmer.

I read the letter through again. Understand I did not, but I was unable to refuse such an intriguing and, I felt, sincere request.

I wrote back to ask Janet Palmer if she would have lunch with me at a small ex-service women's club in South Kensington to which I still belonged. It was quiet and convenient and I felt the ambience would somehow be suitable to the occasion.

One day in the middle of October she met me in the lounge, exactly at 12.45 p.m., as she had promised to do. I judged her to be round about my own age, worn-looking, but once extremely pretty. She was dressed poorly and in an old-fashioned way: a loose tweed coat over a grey suit which might easily have owed its original existence to wartime days.

I asked her if she would like a drink and she accepted, nervously, thanking me right at the start for giving her lunch. I ordered a sherry for us both. It was evident the encounter was a great ordeal for her and I wished I could have done more to make her feel at ease.

'It's really about . . . your brother,' she blurted out, at last.

'My *brother*?'

'Yes.'

The waitress brought our drinks and we both took a sip, rather hurriedly.

'What about him?' I asked. I realised that the occasion was now developing into something difficult for us both.

'Did your mother never tell you? I bore his child.' Her face went scarlet.

I had been looking at her, but to save us both further embarrassment, I looked away. Then, recovering a little, I said, 'No, she never told me.'

'I often wondered,' Janet Palmer went on. 'It's possible that she never even told your father, that it was a secret between us. She preferred to keep her problems to herself. She was that kind of person. But I thought maybe in the end. . . . Look, I don't want to distress you. I swear I'd never have made contact but for . . . unfortunate circumstances.'

'Tell me,' I said, as gently as I could.

'Well, I'll have to go back a long way. It was the spring of 1942. I was in the ATS, as I believe you were, too. Your brother often spoke of you, with great affection. We met when we were both stationed at Headquarters, Southern Command. It was difficult because he was a second lieutenant and I was only a corporal. You know, fraternisation between ranks was frowned upon. But we fell in love. I was in the registry and he was in the Ops room. I was always having to deliver messages to him. Then, quite suddenly, he was posted and almost the next thing I knew was him telephoning me to say he'd been given forty-eight hours' embarkation leave and would I come up to London to spend it with him.'

She paused, obviously finding it hard to go on. We had by now finished our sherries and I ordered two more.

After the waitress had brought them, Janet said, 'Looking back, I sometimes used to wonder whether he was posted because of our association, but then I'd think that was silly because it would have been me who'd have been posted. Anyway, goodness knows how, I managed to get a forty-eight-hour pass and I went up to London. I remember him meeting me at Waterloo, just after he'd been down to Canterbury to say goodbye to your parents. Believe me, Mrs Norbury, I was still a virgin . . . until that last night. I never meant to . . . until I married. But, well, there he was, going abroad to face . . . and I was so in love. There's never been anyone else. I'm still single, but I call myself Mrs Palmer for the sake of my daughter. You see, three weeks after Howard left, I realised I was pregnant.'

'Did you let him know?'

'No. He never knew. I kept putting it off until it was too late. And, after all, what could he have done? All those miles away and going into battle. I just hoped and prayed he'd come through and that the war would end and then we really would get married. I went into labour just after the news of Alamein came on the wireless. Later on, when I heard he'd been killed, I couldn't take it in. They asked me what I wanted to call the baby and I just said "Vera", because Howard and I had been dancing to Vera Lynn singing *We'll Meet Again* the night our child was conceived. Then, when she was christened, I added "Alice".'

'*Alice*?' I broke in, quickly.

'Yes, I'm afraid it doesn't sound quite right after "Vera", but Howard once told me that there was a great-grandmother by that name in your family and that your mother always spoke very highly of her.'

'I see,' I said. So – I had a niece I had known nothing about and Adam had a cousin. 'Did my mother ever meet Vera?' I asked.

'No. Actually, she only met me once, when Vera was small. I think she felt that . . . well . . . she mustn't get too involved, that she ought to keep what had happened as something apart as it would be upsetting for you. You have a little boy now, I believe.'

'Yes, but not so little.' I tried to think back, Alamein. 1942. Good heavens, Howard's daughter would be coming up twenty-one. 'What is Vera doing?' I enquired.

Neither of us was really looking at the other as we spoke, although I was aware of Janet's flush, which had never completely disappeared, now deepening again. Then she said, 'She was a nurse. . . . She'd almost finished her training last summer when it happened.'

I waited. Janet spoke in the past tense. Was Vera dead? If so, I couldn't quite think why her mother wanted to see me. I was soon to know.

'There was this illness, you see. She'd gone to Greece with her boy-friend, well, fiancé really. They intended to get married. They were a lovely couple. They'd joined up with some party or other. They weren't living together, Mrs Norbury. Nothing like that. Vera was a good girl, a dear girl.'

Janet stopped and pulled out a handkerchief, twisting it nervously in her hands. Then she went on, 'She caught this virus. They thought it was 'flu in the beginning. Barry – that was her boy-friend's name – managed to get her on a 'plane and brought her home. I realised it must be serious because he'd told me on the telephone that she'd lost the use of her right leg. I met her at Heathrow with an ambulance.'

This time I stared at Janet, in horror. Thinking of Adam, I said, 'You mean she'd caught . . . polio, or meningitis?'

'No. They never diagnosed either of those things. Although you'd be quite justified in thinking that. But it was something more obscure. She's in a wheel-chair. For life. It's not only her body, though, that's affected. She's mentally . . .'

This time Janet's voice seemed to trail away into complete silence. I was glad we were alone and that everyone else had gone into lunch. When she had recovered a little, I wondered whether we should follow suit, although I couldn't believe either of us would want anything to eat. However, tentatively, I suggested we might make a move to the dining-room and she nodded, accompanying me mutely as we were shown to the table I had reserved which, mercifully, was tucked away in one corner.

Throughout the meal at which, as I suspected, we ate hardly anything, we also conversed little. It was not until we were back in the lounge having coffee, that I asked Janet how Vera was being cared for. I was not in the least surprised when she answered, 'At home. A neighbour's looking after her today. I'll never let her go into an institution. Not as long as I live. It's what I've come about. You've probably guessed.'

'I think so,' I replied. 'Tell me, did my mother . . . ?'

Quickly, she interrupted me. 'In the beginning. Only in the beginning. I wouldn't let her after. She sent me ten pounds every month when Vera was a toddler. God knows how I'd have managed without it. You see, my own mother told me never to darken her doors again. An aunt took pity on us, even though she was as poor as a church mouse and too crippled to look after Vera while I worked. I got typing to do at home. Things like that. Then, at the end of the war, when Vera was three, I went into a clothing factory that was turning out demob suits. It was good pay and there was a crèche for kids. I wrote and told your mother that I could manage then, as I hated not being independent. But she would keep sending. In the end, I came up to London to see her, just like I'm seeing you now, and she finally agreed to stop the payments so long as I promised to let her know if there were any difficulties. She was always very good to us at Christmas and on Vera's birthdays. She was a nice person. I was always hoping we would all meet up one day. I was so proud of Vera. I did so want your mum to see her.'

'Where are you living?'

'In my aunt's council house. She died, but I've been able to keep it on. When Vera went to school all day I got a job as manageress of a laundry and I had some good friends who looked after her until I came home at night and during the holidays. I've always worked although now . . . well, I can't except for casual typing and such like.'

I did some quick mental arithmetic. Even if it meant not being able to buy Maplethorpe if and when it came up for sale, this woman before me, who might so easily have been my legal sister-in-law, had had one of the worst deals that life could possibly have handed out. And whereas my son had recovered – or all but – from a dreaded illness, Janet's daughter had been crippled mentally and physically for life. Yet she had struggled on with the utmost courage and she would go on doing so as long as she drew breath. I reckoned it must have cost her quite a lot to come and see me today, also that she wouldn't have done so if she hadn't been pretty desperate.

What was more, I was fairly sure now that, although my mother had never known about the final appalling tragedy, it must have been Janet Palmer and her daughter about whom she had been thinking when she had said she wished to make a codicil to her will.

'Would fifty a month,' I asked Janet, 'help?'

10

I write today with a heavy heart. Tragedy has struck at two families in the village, one high, one low, namely the Dewhursts at the Hall and Widow Shergold in her little cottage by the mill. Would that I could help but, alas, I fear there is nothing anyone can do and, indeed, there is no actual confirmation as to what exactly has happened, nor is there ever likely to be. I am only in possession of a few known facts which, sadly, appear to point to what surely must be the truth.

The eldest Dewhurst son, who was to have gone into the Horse Guards, has suddenly been sent to Australia. When Shiner, our groom, went to Overley station to collect my brother, Harry, who was coming to stay, he caught sight of the Honourable Frank getting out of the family brougham along with several suitcases and a trunk. Shiner's sharp eyes noticed the address on the latter: some sheep farm in New South Wales. A few days prior to this, Percy Shergold told Cook that his eldest sister, Bessie, who had recently been taken on as a housemaid at the Hall, had been dismissed without notice and had gone to live with an uncle and aunt in the north of the county. I would not have heard all this but for Miss Clutterbuck, to whom Cook is apt to talk when she takes her a cup of tea in Mamma's old room. Miss C. is making me some splendid sheets, all hem-stitched and embroidered with my initials. Amongst many another piece of material which Mamma left, I discovered some lovely Irish linen which lasts for ever.

Poor Lady Dewhurst, poor Widow Shergold, poor Bessie and her unborn child. I can't seem to get them out of my mind. I suppose the baby will be adopted. Mother Barnes, the mid-wife, would help in this respect. She knows about foster parents. Of course, whatever happens, the Dewhursts will be bound to pay.

Perhaps it is a blessing that I have only girls, who are being brought up in such a way that they would be unlikely ever to find themselves in such a vulnerable position as poor Bessie

Shergold. They will always be well chaperoned and not at the mercy of young men without the strength of character to curb their natural desires. Each night, I go down on my knees and thank God for my good fortune in having such a wonderful family.

Well said, Alice. She knew about life all right. And human nature. And she wasn't a prude or all that censorious. She hadn't really laid any blame at the doorstep of either the Dewhursts' son or Bessie Shergold. Her compassion embraced every participant in this sad little saga.

And hadn't my own mother shown, within limits, compassion in respect of poor Janet Palmer? She had not behaved as Janet's own mother had done, even if she had never actually *seen* Vera. I kept thinking about the reasons for this. Had she been afraid that my father would have been deeply shocked? Had she wanted Howard's image to remain untarnished, both in his eyes and mine? Of course, later on, when Adam came on the scene, she would probably have found it even more difficult to divulge the truth. She would have wanted him to think of his dead uncle as a hero, beyond reproach. How I longed to be able to ring her up and ask. I'm sure she acted for what she felt was the best under incredibly difficult circumstances. I recalled how she had never stopped grieving over Howard's death; how, when I went home on leave I would catch her staring at his photograph; how it seemed as if there were times when she almost wanted to talk to me about her feelings – rather as I had sensed she had wanted to say something during her last illness – and then, in the end, decided to remain silent.

Somehow, I felt infinitely proud of my forebears, sad that I had not tried to understand my mother better, had not appreciated the way she dealt with her own troubles without pushing the burden on to anyone else. I would never know more about her now. I was a daughter who had failed. I had thought I had known best as to how to help her after my father died, but I'd made a pretty poor job of it. From somewhere in the recesses of my mind I remembered reading that a younger generation always *thinks* it knows the answers, that it is clued up and quite different from the previous generation, but that this wasn't true. The writer had gone on to say that we're all alike, we all find out the same things in the end and then, when we've done that, it's time to bow out. I came to the conclusion that, thanks to Great-Granny Alice, I was certainly finding out a thing or two, but I had a long way to go before I could acquire a fraction of her wisdom or that of my mother's. Perhaps I never would. All the same, I meant to have a jolly good try. I hoped I wouldn't bow out for a while.

Just at the moment, I seemed to have so much to do. I was committed in so many different ways. Adam was constantly in my mind, even though he was away at school. Then there was the clearing up of my mother's Estate, Great-Granny Alice's diaries to edit and now this new unexpected development: poor Janet Palmer and her stricken daughter. Guiltily, I suddenly realised that George was nowhere in my list and my mother's words came back to me 'Men need more than mere catering for, Vicky'. I had forgiven him for the stand he had taken during her last illness knowing, in my heart of hearts, that I had much to answer for and that, if I were really honest with myself, I had found the business of getting my mother cared for in her own home, harrowing as it seemed, probably the wisest course. Had I known then about George's fear of cancer, I would have realised that having my mother at Ackerley would have been quite out of the question.

Hastily, now, I switched my priorities round: Adam, George, Janet and Vera, my mother's Estate, Great-Granny Alice – although I disliked putting her last. Every day she became more and more real and important to me. I turned to her for solace in a way that I had never turned – or thought I could never turn – to my mother.

I wondered whether to tell George about Janet Palmer but, for the time being at any rate, decided against it. I wasn't quite sure why, except that I thought he might possibly disapprove of my handing out fifty pounds a month and I did not want to jeopardise our improved relationship. I had no clear idea how I had arrived at this sum, nor had I any exact knowledge, at this stage, of how much my mother had left. That she had always been frugal and had spent hardly anything on herself, there was no doubt. After death duties had been paid and I had received my two thousand, sold her flat and possibly a few of her goods and chattels, I imagined the Trust for Adam, as the main beneficiary, might come to between ten and fifteen thousand. Not for the first time, I wished she had confided in me about the codicil she was never able to make. I felt fairly certain now that it would have been in favour of Janet Palmer and had my mother not died before Vera's accident it might well have been a more substantial bequest; for, however much my mother might have denied herself, she had always been generous and charitable to others, apart from people, such as Miss Fisk, who she felt had been taking advantage of her.

Fortunately, thanks to George and an earlier small legacy from a godmother, I had accumulated quite a little nest egg over the years, although this had naturally been somewhat depleted of late by my insistence on paying my mother's private medical and nursing-home fees and subsidising her various companions. I think she remained happily unaware of this latter state of affairs and I was glad this was so. If she had known that I had ever slipped cash into the hands of Miss Fisk and her successors, she would have been angry and horrified. But thanks to my own tendency to save, probably fostered by the remembrance of the depression in my youth, I reckoned that my finances were still in reasonable shape. I felt, in fact, extremely lucky and, when I thought of poor Janet Palmer and Vera, guilty as well. Perhaps, like Alice, I was a conservative with socialist tendencies. I thought how nice it would be if wealth could be evened out, although I knew that in practice it never seemed to work. But hard luck stories always moved me, especially when it was so obvious that the afflicted were utterly deserving. For the next few weeks I went about my various tasks – mostly in connection with my mother's affairs – a little desperately, hoping for the best.

Taking time off with George to go down to Adam's school one Sunday in order to give him and Julian Wainwright an outing was a splendid respite. In a matter of weeks our son appeared to have filled out, acquired a new assurance and his friend was delightful. I sent up a small prayer, rather as Great-Granny Alice had done, for my good fortune. I also resolved that I would shortly pay a visit not only to the Tanners but also that valiant woman and her daughter, to whom Adam and I were indirectly related.

Unfortunately, an epidemic of influenza to which both George and I succumbed rather badly, followed by the approach of Christmas, prevented me from carrying out either intention until later in the New Year. I planned to leave early one Friday, Alaric Reed having promised to show me the parish records at eleven a.m., and I told George I would be home on Sunday night – although not that I would be making rather a long detour via Southampton on the way.

'You're really hooked on Alice, aren't you?' he said, the night before I left.

'Sort of, I suppose.'

'I'm glad. I began to wonder how you'd make out with Adam away and your mother gone.'

Then he said something which took me by complete surprise. 'You've never really liked it here, have you, Vicky? Being the wife of a club secretary's not exactly your scene.'

I became embarrassed. It was so unlike him to embark on any kind of soul-searching conversation.

I hedged. 'I'm not very convivial, I must admit. I expect you've often wished I was, well . . . more like Jack Pinner's wife.'

His eyes opened wide. '*Sylvia Pinner*? What ever makes you say that?'

'I've no idea, except . . . she's good at a party.'

He got up to pour himself another whisky. 'Jack Pinner is welcome to Sylvia,' he replied, over his shoulder.

I thought of his remark as I drove to Ivers. Why on earth had I picked on Sylvia Pinner as a comparison? Sylvia, with her so obviously dyed hair, baby doll image and tinkling laugh. Could it be because the night we got home after taking Adam to school for the start of his second term, we had dined in the club and the Pinners had been sitting next to us? Afterwards, George had suggested that they should come up to our apartment for a night-cap. I hadn't really wanted them, for I was tired and also sad at saying goodbye to Adam again, even though I knew he was more than happy to be back with his contemporaries, particularly Julian. The other reason was that when I had drunk wine, as I had that evening, I never liked a night-cap. Mixing drinks invariably gave me a headache the following morning. After we got upstairs, I simply asked George for a squash and found Sylvia's 'Oh, go on, Vicky, be a devil,' somehow extremely irritating. I refrained from mentioning the reason for my abstinence because it seemed so feeble. I just shook my head and said that a soft drink was really all I wanted.

I recalled that the talk had then turned, inevitably, to holidays. Jack and Sylvia were going skiing at St Moritz and I think it was Jack who suggested that we might go with them. 'You never seem to get away, George,' I remember him saying. 'Don't the powers that be let you off the hook sometimes?'

George had given a slow smile. 'Oh yes, they certainly would give me a holiday if I wanted one but . . . well, I prefer to stay here. Besides, can you see me taking up skiing at my time of life and carrying this kind of weight?'

There had been general laughter in which I had joined in. Now, driving off to Ivers, I suddenly wondered whether we had all been rather unkind. And perhaps I was being more unkind in pushing off for a weekend on such an incredibly personal pursuit, which wouldn't have interested George in the least. I simply wasn't the right wife for him, any more, I suppose, than he was the right husband for me. Yet, in many ways, we were on a more even keel these days. We'd had our ups and downs, especially the latter during my mother's illness, but we'd come through. Adam was happy and settled at boarding-school, my mother's affairs were all but wound up, I had this big new literary interest and George . . .

I stopped at some traffic lights. Unfortunately, I couldn't think of any extra pleasure which George might have. But he *seemed* happy enough.

11

Alaric was already in the vestry when I arrived, kneeling beside an enormous oak chest. He stood up and brushed himself down.

'I don't think I'll offer to shake hands,' he said, 'these old papers are in a pretty dusty state. As a matter of fact, I'm awfully glad you've galvanised me into action about them, because after you've finished having a look I'm going to get them transferred to the county record office. It's where they ought to be, but I've been so busy I haven't got around to sending them there. I think I've already dug out quite a bit of information about your Percy and the Medway family. Of course, it's only simple facts like baptisms, marriages and burials. If you want certificates and things like that you'll have to go to Somerset House. Actually, I reckon you'd get much more low-down, as it were, if you visited old Kate Moon at *The Plough and Sickle*.'

'Kate Moon?' I queried.

'Yes. She's the mother of the present publican, Dickie Moon. Known as the Duchess. She's about sixty. Lives with Dickie and his wife and gives them pretty good hell, I believe. You don't want to get the wrong side of her, but if she likes you she'll come across. Aristocratic-looking old thing. Anyway, she knows a lot about the village and seems to have been related to some Shergold or other, way back.'

'You seem to be pretty well informed about your parishioners,' I said.

'Well, it's what I'm here for, isn't it? Human beings. In the old days, I suppose I'd have called them my flock. Damned impertinent, really. But I do wish I knew more about them. What with babies being born and everyone living longer, it's hard to keep track of three parishes. I'd like to give you more time today, because I think family histories are fascinating.' He glanced at his watch. 'Look, how about my leaving you to it and coming back just before one? You said the Tanners were expecting you for lunch and they've kindly invited me too. By then you'll probably be able to tell whether you want to go on delving about here this afternoon or prefer to go walkabout. I hope you won't be perished. I've lit this paraffin heater, but it's not awfully efficient.'

'That seems like a splendid idea. And I've come prepared for the cold.'

He went away and I was alone in what I could only think of as Great-Granny Alice's church. It was very still, except for the rustle of paper as I turned over the documents. Here, before me, was the actual past. I was touching it, sensing it, savouring its musty, faint, yet all-pervading perfume. Here were the records of generations who had lived and loved and had their being in a neighbourhood outside of which many of them had scarcely set foot.

I noted both Alice's and Lionel's demise and those of two spinster daughters, who had evidently cared for their father after their mother's death and who had probably seen to all the arrangements for my grandmother Hannah's wedding. I discovered the respective dates of the deaths of the Earl and Countess of Dewhurst. Then I found something very intriguing: the marriage of a Bessie Shergold to an Arthur Silverthorne in March 1878. Presumably, someone had taken on the fallen Bessie, together with her child who had been fathered by another man. There had been no need for adoption. I wondered what had happened to the Honourable Frank. And who was Arthur Silverthorne?

I could not begin to go through all the records confronting me and, in any case, I realised that many names in which I was interested could well be in the records of more distant parishes. And how much did they matter to my main objective? Certainly, they must have mattered a great deal to a variety of people when such individuals had been alive. I thought of all the agonising that Widow Shergold must have gone through, when she knew her eldest daughter was pregnant out of wedlock and how pleased she must have been when Arthur Silverthorne had made an honest woman of Bessie in the end. Would Frank have known about this or had he simply lain low in New South Wales and made another life for himself? And what about his parents? After their initial anger, fear and disappointment had they disinherited him in favour of their second son, the one whose boots Great-Granny Alice had bought for Percy? Had they been able to put Frank out of their minds, shrug off a youthful indiscretion as something which could simply be settled by a cash hand-out? Had the fact that, somewhere along the line, they had an illegitimate grandson or granddaughter meant nothing to them? I must remember to make some enquiries about the Dewhurst family. I only knew that at some period they had sold up and the Hall was now an institution for the physically disabled.

Thinking of the likelihood of the Dewhursts getting out of their responsibilities merely by paying, made me suddenly angry. I had, of course, no proof. I had allowed my imagination to run away with me. Yet the thought of my brother, Howard, somehow paying with his life for making Janet Palmer pregnant came into my mind. Then I realised that this was muddled thinking. Howard had given his life for his country. He had never known about the new life he had generated. It was Janet who had paid and was now still paying one of the highest prices I could think of in terms of self-sacrifice. And she had never married, like Bessie Shergold, never had the support of a husband in what must have been those long lonely years bringing up Vera.

I wondered about the other children Arthur Silverthorne and Bessie had probably had, whether he had been a good stepfather, why, exactly, he had married her. Had his feelings been aroused by her physical charms, pity for her plight or – and here, I fear, a certain cynicism crept into my mind – the money which the Dewhursts had allowed her? I had no idea what was usual in such circumstances. Would it have been a lump sum or income? If the child was to be adopted, I imagined it might have been the former. On the other hand, income would have seemed much more sensible from the donor's point of view. The status of the recipient could so easily alter, as, indeed, it had in Bessie's case, when there would appear to be no further need for maintenance.

Alaric arrived a little before one, just as he had promised. He found me sitting on a hassock by the open chest deep in thought, a few papers on the floor beside me. There was, I realised, a limit to how long one could go on researching and I felt a visit to Kate Moon might be a pleasant diversion that afternoon.

After lunch at Ivers, at which both Prue and her husband, Peter – who was home on leave for a few days – could hardly have been more welcoming or entertaining, I set off with Alaric for *The Plough and Sickle*. We arrived after closing-time and Alaric who, despite remarks to the contrary, seemed to know quite a bit about his parishioners and their habits, asked me to follow him round to the back entrance where he banged on the door.

A voluptuous fair-haired woman of about forty answered it, wearing a pair of fashionable fawn trousers and a bright, rather too tight, orange sweater.

'Why, Rector . . . It's not often you visit *The Plough* after hours. But come on in out of the cold. I've just made a pot of tea. Perhaps you'd both like a cup?' She smiled at me and we moved inside, Alaric effecting introductions meanwhile.

'It's Ma you'll be wanting to talk to,' she said, after she had heard what we had come about. 'She'll love that. She's always on about the past. I'll give her a call. She's gone up to have a bit of a kip. Says it's the only time she can get one, when the bar's closed.'

'Oh, please don't . . .' I began, but it was too late.

In response to a raucous shout of, 'Ma, there's a lady down here who I think you'd like to see,' a tall grey-haired woman soon joined us. I could quite understand why she had been nicknamed the Duchess. There was something definitely aristocratic about Mrs Moon senior, something haughty, almost disdainful about the way she looked at me out of her penetrating blue eyes as we shook hands.

'Mrs Norbury, here, is researching into the parish records, Mrs Moon,' Alaric said. 'I felt you, of all people, know so much about the district and its inhabitants. Also I believe you once mentioned you were related to the Shergolds.'

Kate Moon inclined her head. 'That is correct, Rector.' Then she turned to me and enquired, 'And which of the Shergolds are you most interested in, Mrs Norbury? There's a lot of them about.'

We were, by now, sitting at the kitchen table and Mrs Moon's daughter-in-law had passed round cups of tea. I felt all at once rather foolish. Here was I, wasting the time of a whole lot of people whom I hardly knew, being given bed and board, the freedom of the parish records, just in order to satisfy my curiosity. And for what? I didn't really know. I had no idea whether a book based on Great-Granny Alice's diaries would ever see print. For all I knew, it might be consigned to some drawer, my son might be as uninterested in Alice as I had once been and George would certainly never want to read the manuscript. I was simply an interfering old busybody. It was if I'd thrown a pebble into the mill-pond I had espied on walking through the village and the ripples simply wouldn't stop rippling. But they were all looking at me now. I had to say something.

'Towards the end of the last century,' I faltered, 'there was a little boy called Percy, who died in the early nineteen-thirties.'

'My grandmother's brother, Mrs Norbury,' replied Mrs Moon senior, promptly. 'Started work at the age of ten. Pity the young of today aren't made to do likewise.' She spoke proudly, defiantly, giving her daughter-in-law a meaningful glance as she did so.

The words were out of my mouth before I could stop them. 'Was it your grandmother,' I asked, 'who married an Arthur Silverthorne?'

Again, there came that regal inclination of the head, much more dignified than a simple nod.

'Yes, Mrs Norbury. My mother was their *eldest* child.'

The inflexion on *eldest* was unmistakable. She looked at me even more defiantly now. I knew that she knew that I knew that I was talking to the granddaughter of the Honourable Frank's by-blow.

12

*There has been grievous news from Germany for our beloved
Queen. The whole nation is deeply shocked. In today's Morning
Post we have learnt that her daughter, Alice – my namesake –
has died from the dreadful disease which has already carried off
the rest of her family: diphtheria. How I pray, daily, that my
own dear ones may be spared. It is this damp time of year when
the scourge is always at its worst. I stopped the children being
taken anywhere near the mill cottages on their walks, for last
month poor Widow Shergold's youngest was carried off in the
fever van to the isolation hospital and died within three days.
It is a mercy none of her others succumbed. She has had enough
of her share of troubles, poor thing. At least she must be relieved
that Bessie has married and moved nearer home again. They
say her husband, Arthur Silverthorne, is a most hard-working
man. Having been a cooper for a brewery firm in Swindon, he
has now started up his own business in Overley. I understand
the baby thrives and that Bessie is expecting again.*

And now to think, I had just met Bessie's grand-daughter.
I was caught up in something beyond my control, a pawn
in a game of chance which was exciting and which I did
not want to end.

Yet suddenly it did not seem quite so exciting, when I
reached the outskirts of Southampton and began driving
down some mean streets near the docks, looking out for
the one where Janet Palmer lived. At last I found it,
managed to park the car not far away and walked back to
Number Three, Jubilee Terrace, where I knocked on the
door. I had said I would call between five and five thirty,
a time when I hoped Janet would not feel obliged to offer
me any refreshment, but to my consternation I saw tea
already spread out on the front-room table, a meal over
which she had obviously taken a great deal of trouble.

'Thank you,' she said, 'for coming,' rather as she had thanked me for giving her lunch in London before she had hardly sat down. There was no sign of Vera except for her bed made up in one corner, but her mother went on to say that a neighbour – the one who had looked after her daughter when Janet had come to see me – had taken her out in her wheel-chair and they would be back shortly. I sensed that perhaps Janet wanted a little time with me alone.

'It's so kind of you . . .' she continued. I wished she wouldn't be so wretchedly grateful. It made me feel acutely embarrassed and I wondered whether my visit was really such a bright idea after all. Should I perhaps just ante up the fifty pounds monthly or give her some lump sum? Not for the first time did I reflect that it was all very well for the nation to have been told that it had never had it so good, but I would have thought such words must have sounded a bit hollow in the ears of Janet Palmer. I noticed a small typewriter in a corner of the room and she was quick to follow my gaze.

'I still do a bit of typing in the evenings, like I used to when Vera was a baby. Of course, it's not like it was in the war days, when firms were only too glad to find a bit of part-time help. I expect you remember, there were only those wretched stencils then. No copying machines. Sometimes, I can't think how everyone managed without them. Now, business is all so technical, electric typewriters, computers, the lot. But if you can find any authors who want manuscripts typed, that's different. I'm a bit rusty, but so long as you can read their writing, they don't mind the odd mistake. And it's an interest, apart from anything else, with Vera being how she is.'

A thought occurred to me. 'Would you be prepared to do some typing for me? I'm editing, or, rather, trying to edit, my great-grandmother's diaries and putting in linking passages here and there. At the moment I'm still at the stage of getting it all together, so to speak, but in a little while I think I probably could do with some fair copies.'

'Why, *yes*.' Her face visibly brightened. 'I'd love to help when I've finished the book I'm on. Only I wouldn't want to be paid. I'd do it for free. You've given me quite enough already.'

'Don't talk rubbish. This would be strictly business. The trouble is I wouldn't want to trust the diaries and manuscript to the post. Perhaps I could bring them down to you some time. I'd know then that everything was in safe hands.'

'Of course. I'd take the greatest care of whatever you left with me.' All at once, her expression changed, as a wheel-chair passed the window and she jumped up to open the front door.

I don't really know what I was expecting exactly, certainly not quite such a pathetic creature as Janet pushed into the living-room, whose head seemed permanently tilted to one side and whose eyes did not seem to register my presence, when her mother said, 'This is Mrs Norbury, Vera.'

As there was no answer, I went forward and held the girl's hand, because that seemed the only thing to do.

'I'll make the tea,' Janet said quickly, and disappeared leaving me alone with her daughter who, to my surprise, suddenly swivelled her wheel-chair round and stared at me, suspiciously, before saying something which sounded like 'Visitor' or it may have been 'Is it her?'

'My name's Vicky,' I said hopefully. 'I know your mother.'

There was silence. I wished Janet would come back. I began to panic. I felt I wanted to shout, 'And I knew your father *very* well. He was my brother. You're really my niece.' I wondered what Howard would say if he could see us all now.

'Well, here's the cup that cheers,' said Janet, brightly, at last returning, to my great relief, with the teapot. She pushed Vera's chair close to the table and began pouring out.

I thought of the cosiness of Ivers which I had just left and the luxury of Ackerley to which I was suddenly longing to get back. You're spoilt, something inside me kept saying.

You can't take this. You shouldn't have come. You're simply getting involved in something to assuage your own guilt and it's made you feel worse. Your mother handled the situation better. She was no fool. You're just a meddler, meddling in the past and now the present. And wasn't it rather condescending and insensitive of you to ask this poor woman to type a story with some rather delicate bits? She might start comparing herself to Bessie Shergold and, so far, Bessie seems to have done so much better for herself.

I did my best to make conversation. I asked Janet more about the author for whom she typed, how long since her aunt had died, her job as a manageress of a laundry, what Southampton had been like in the blitz.

We conversed, literally, over and above Vera's head. I was relieved to find that the girl could at least eat unaided and appeared to be enjoying her tea. Although I had no appetite, partly because of all Prue Tanner's sumptuous hospitality but mostly because of the distressing situation in which I now found myself, I managed to do justice to a large slice of Janet's homemade sandwich cake, on which I complimented her.

It had become dark outside and a flurry of snowflakes spattered against the window. Janet jumped up and switched on the second bar of the electric fire in the grate. 'I suppose we must expect this sort of weather now,' she said. 'I remember how my mother used to say, "As the days lengthen, the cold strengthens".'

I longed to ask her whether her mother was still alive, but Janet forestalled me. She seemed to be such a strange mixture of trite remarks, yet acute sensitivity. I guessed it was sheer nervousness which probably accounted for the former.

'My mother passed on three years ago,' she volunteered.

'Did she . . .?' I began, looking across at Vera, but the girl seemed quite oblivious to anything we were talking about.

'Yes, she softened', Janet said, 'sort of came round a bit in the end. She was very proud of Vera being a nurse. You'll never believe this but she died in Southampton

General in the very ward that Vicky was on. Queer how life turns out, isn't it?'

'Yes,' I answered. It was certainly queer, all right.

As soon as I could after tea, I made my departure.

'Your work . . .?' Janet asked, escorting me to the door. I had almost forgotten about it.

'Oh, yes, of course. How long do you think your present author will need you?'

'I should think another month might see it through. Of course, there's all the tidying up and that, and he's a bit apt to alter. You know, pernickety about his phrasing. But he won't start on anything new for a while.'

She promised to let me know how things went and thanked me again profusely for all I was doing.

On my way home I couldn't get the scene I had just witnessed out of my mind. I thought of Howard and what would have happened supposing he had not been killed and he and Janet had married. Would they have made a go of things and, after twenty-one years, still have been together? Would the disparity between their respective backgrounds have proved too much for them in the end, finally extinguishing the sexual desire which had brought them together? Surely Janet's cliché-ridden conversation would have exasperated my brother after a while? Or would she have improved herself, adapted to his way of life? She was by no means unintelligent but, sadly, circumstances had always been against her, preventing her from stretching that intelligence.

Suddenly, I checked myself. What an appalling despicable little snob I was being. Perhaps it was fortunate that, at this juncture, the snow really began to come down and I was obliged to concentrate on my driving. It was a long slow journey because the conditions rapidly worsened. I had told George that I hoped to be back around eight p.m. and, as it got nearer that time, I looked out rather hopelessly for a telephone box. But even when I managed, just, to catch sight of one, the cars before and behind me precluded my trying to stop. In the end I gave up. He would surely know that the weather was responsible for my lateness.

I did not get home until well past ten. On opening the front door of our apartment, I saw a large piece of paper on the hall table held in place by the telephone. On it was written: *1.45 p.m. Adam has suspected appendicitis. Tried to contact you at Ivers but heard you had had an early lunch and already left to visit a friend on the way home. Thought it best to get on down to the school. Will let you know the form. Love, George.*

I tore off my gloves. Before I had had time to dial, the instrument beside me began ringing: piercing, demanding and, in my exhausted overwrought state, somehow totally menacing.

My hand shook as I picked up the receiver.

13

My anxiety, mercifully, was short-lived. Adam's suspected appendicitis turned out to be a false alarm. George's telephone call – after several earlier ones, I later learnt – was to say that although the child had been taken to the local hospital, his temperature had miraculously dropped to normal. He went on to say that he would ring me again in the morning, spend the night in the hotel we often used when visiting the school and, if Adam was pronounced fit to return there, he himself would drive straight back to Ackerley. He told me not to worry, to get some sleep and that everything was under control. He also added that he was glad I was safely home in such appalling weather conditions. He did not mention or enquire about the 'friend' on whom the Tanners had said I intended to call.

I had to hand it to my husband. He *was* efficient. He would never have been made an ADC if not. A club secretary in peacetime mightn't sound all that grand, but there was no doubt he was a very good one, that he had a flair for organisation and keeping people happy and had turned Ackerley into one of the most popular places of its kind in southern England. Moreover, he had gone off at once to Adam's school as soon as he had heard that our son was ill. Besides, when he returned at lunchtime the following day, he could so easily have said, 'Who the hell were you calling on?' He simply reported that Adam was fine again, so that I somehow felt I owed it to my husband to tell him about Janet Palmer.

'Strewth, Vicky,' he said. 'You don't half get yourself *involved*, don't you. Did your mother have any proof?'

'Proof?' It had never occurred to me to think about proof and I am sure it had never occurred to her either. Having met Janet Palmer, she was so palpably genuine. I was rather shocked by George's immediate reaction, even though he did not sound angry or censorious. I suppose that men's minds always work rather differently from women's in cases like this.

'There's no need for proof,' I answered. 'Janet's a terribly nice person who's had a frightfully raw deal.'

'Yes, I expect you're right.' He spoke quite kindly now. 'It's just that you do rather tend to go into things head first, Vicky. Sort of rush your fences, so to speak. Is there any chance that the situation might improve?'

'I can't see it doing so. The daughter's wrecked for life. Social security doesn't add up to all that much. Janet's had to give up her job and she's vowed never to let Vera go into a home – at least, only over her dead body. It's . . . well, one of the most tragic cases I can think of.'

He was silent. Then he said, 'Yes, I understand. Under normal circumstances, I suppose Vera would have married, her mother would never have approached you and you'd never have known anything about either of them.'

'No.'

'I wonder,' he remarked, 'just how many other young illegitimate people of Vera's age are kicking around at the moment as a result of the war years.'

It was something I'd never really thought about. Now, it seemed obvious there must be a very high number. The doctors hadn't come up with the pill in those days. The copying machines, to which Janet had referred, were not the only advantage that would have made a considerable difference if they had been around between 1939 and 1945. George and I had been lucky – not that I'd ever slept with him before marriage – but we had planned not to bring a child into the world until peace came and, initially, I had only him to thank for taking care of that side of things. Then, for some reason, Adam didn't come along until 1949.

Suddenly, my husband said, 'How are your finances, old thing? Even with your mother's legacy, fifty pounds a month is going to make quite a hole in them, isn't it? One way and another, you've had quite a few expenses lately.'

'Yes, but I can manage. I've never been extravagant.'

'No. You've never been that.'

My birthday was coming up soon and I was touched when I discovered that George had doubled the figure on the cheque he usually gave me, saying 'Jack Pinner put me on to a pretty good investment a little while ago. Let's say the extra is for charity.' Other than his attitude when my mother had been ill, George had always been chari- table. I tried not to think that there might be any feelings of guilt over my mother connected with my latest present.

It was just before the Easter holidays when I went to see Janet again, bringing with me as much material as I had got together. Even though I knew she would take the greatest care of the diaries, her mention of copying machines had prompted me to get the marked pages photocopied. It was an expensive measure, but every day I was beginning to feel more and more that I was in possession of something unique, that its loss – at least to me – would be devastating. At a pinch, I might just be able to re-write my own script. I could never re-write Great-Granny Alice's diaries.

Only the day before I had come across:

August 1st, 1879

This has been the worst summer ever recorded. It has rained continuously. Everywhere the harvest is blackened and farmers faced with ruin. The Morning Post has reported three million sheep dying of liver-fluke. Lionel is desperately worried. Poor Mr Disraeli – or I suppose I should say, the Earl of Beaconsfield – is being hounded by his opponents. But he cannot be held responsible for the weather, nor the railways pushing further and further into the Canadian prairies and cheap wheat flooding the British market. I hear that Percy has been tempted by Bessie to leave Ivers, as her husband could give him a better-paid job in his own business, which at least is one that is expanding. I do hope the boy won't leave. He is such a good worker, although Lionel cannot possibly afford to pay him more than ten shillings a week.

I found the clarity, erudition and faithful reporting in Great-Granny Alice's diaries quite extraordinary. She was no ordinary farmer's wife, only concerned with her family and servants. She took a positive interest in her husband's affairs, his employees and the world at large. This last entry prompted me to look back to what she had written about her upbringing. I had become aware that Mamma had been the only child of a well-to-do west country clothier – no wonder Alice had found so many yards of good material amongst her goods and chattels – who had married and, I suspect, probably financed, a handsome husband called Freddie, who appeared to have been something of a dilettante. Nevertheless, Mamma's shrewd and businesslike father had evidently seen to it that his daughter's dowry was tied up in such a way that she and her children were never in want. Indeed, a governess had been employed who must have been a cut above the ordinary. Great-Granny Alice had written at one stage: *I try to think of the less fortunate members of society. I remember so well how Miss Hardy-Macdonald used to talk to us about Lord Shaftesbury and all he was doing to prevent little children being so persecuted in the mines.*

I could quite understand Great-Granny Alice's interest in Percy. She was a woman ahead of her times. I again wondered whether she felt she was writing for posterity. Fancifully, it occurred to me that she might have had second sight, a feeling that eighty years on some greenhorn of a descendant might try to bring her words to the public eye. I wished I had half her wisdom, talent and dedication.

I said something of this sort to Janet Palmer when I found myself sitting once more in her little front room at Jubilee Terrace.

'Why do you underrate yourself so much?' she asked.

In spite of her seeming humility, somewhere or other there was a shrewdness about her, an underlying strength which had obviously brought her through untold vicissitudes.

'I don't know,' I answered. 'I just feel Great-Granny Alice had something in her that I don't possess.'

'I wouldn't be too sure of that,' she said, glancing at the pile of foolscap I had brought with me.

I realised that there had been a shift in our relationship. I thought of Janet now as an ally, someone who wanted to support me, join forces and show an interest in what I was trying to do. She was no mere typist. After all, she

would be taking part in a journey of discovery into her
daughter's ancestors, even if the unfortunate girl was so
afflicted and had been born on what moralists still call 'the
wrong side of the blanket'.

Poor Vera. She seemed just the same, sitting in a corner
of the room in her wheel-chair, occasionally making unintelligible – at least, to me – noises, but which her mother
appeared able to interpret, as if the two of them were in
communication even if a third party was left completely in
the dark.

'Shall you be getting an agent?' Janet enquired, as I got
up to go.

'An agent?' I suppose I must have looked at her rather
stupidly. I simply hadn't got that far in my scheme of
things. There was such a long way to go yet.

'All the authors I've worked for have had agents,' Janet
continued. 'They find them useful about contracts and
things.' She mentioned one or two by name.

I had not even thought about a contract. I was still doing
what I felt to be necessary with the diaries, acting, I
suppose, on instinct, going about my self-appointed task
in a completely amateurish fashion.

'I'll think about what you say,' I replied. 'It sounds a bit
grand, though, to feel I might need an agent.'

Yet on my way home the idea of taking Janet's advice
kept returning. So far, in my eagerness, I realised I had
just pressed on regardless. What was it George had said
when I had first told him about Janet Palmer? 'You do
rather rush your fences, Vicky.'

The thought that perhaps I did need help was reinforced
a few days later when I read Great-Granny Alice's entry
for February 6th, 1880.

*It will soon be Lady Day. Lionel has gone to the Estate Office
to see the Earl's agent, Mr Ponsonby. So far, he has been
putting off such an encounter, but he feels the time has come
when he is obliged to ask for a reduction in rent, particularly
as the long-awaited promise of repairs to the barn has not been
fulfilled. Although Henry Ponsonby naturally has the Earl's
interests at heart, Lionel has always felt him a most reasonable*

*man to deal with. How I hope and pray there will be a
satisfactory outcome.*

Yes, maybe agents were necessary, after all: diplomatic
go-betweens who smoothed the path between landlord
and tenant, author and publisher, reconciling the needs of
each to their mutual advantage. After the Easter holidays
I decided that I would get in touch with one or other of
the firms which Janet Palmer had recommended.

14

Miss Ruby Thetford was not all the kind of literary agent I had imagined her to be, when I was ushered into her office in High Holborn in the middle of a June heat-wave. Although Janet had never met her, she had assured me, when handing over my immaculately typed manuscript, that the last author for whom she worked had found Ruby most sympathetic and helpful and had given him many constructive ideas. I thought perhaps Ruby got on better with men than women, or maybe I had caught her on a bad day; but whatever it was I felt she and I had got off to a bad start. Ruby sat there behind her desk piled high with papers and books: a little dark-eyed woman, with a fringe and large owlish spectacles, through which she peered at me, almost, it seemed, suspiciously.

'According to your letter, I understand you have diaries written by a relative in the latter half of the last century.'

'Yes. My great-grandmother's.'

'What makes you think they are publishable?'

'I . . .' Why did I think they were publishable? Maybe they weren't. I didn't know. That was what I had come to find out, hadn't I? 'I . . . found them interesting myself,' I replied, rather lamely.

'But it is *your* ancestor. She would naturally be of more interest to you, if you see what I mean. Look at the people who are always trying to trace their family history, when they wouldn't care a jot about anyone else's.'

'Yes, but my great-grandmother seems to me to have been unusual. She has given a very fair and vivid picture of the times in which she lived. I've picked out entries which I consider to be the most apposite and linked them with passages of my own, doing a little comparing with the present day as I went along.' I was amazed at my sudden assertiveness. I suppose I was like a mother defending her child.

Ruby Thetford frowned. 'Is that the completed tome?' she enquired, looking at the parcel I held rather awkwardly on my lap.

'Er . . . no. I'm only half-way through, actually. I just thought the time had come to seek professional advice.'

'I see. From the size of what you have there it seems to me that you already have a book. But then all books are usually too long. Need cutting,' she ended, abruptly.

I thought of someone, perhaps Ruby, blue-pencilling my every page. I suppose I must have looked rather miserable because suddenly she said, 'Don't worry. Skilfully done, it can be a great improvement. Anyway, leave the stuff with me and I'll let you know what I think. But don't expect to hear for a while. I'm going on holiday very soon and I'm already pledged to take three other manuscripts with me to read.'

I went back to Ackerley and tried to contain my soul in patience. But it wasn't easy. My interview with Ruby had made it more or less impossible to continue with my task. If she was going to write back and say I had been wasting my time, there was no point in pressing ahead at the moment. I occupied myself with various mundane jobs about the flat and buying Adam some new clothes, as on each occasion we saw him he seemed to have filled out in all directions.

I still had heard nothing from Ruby when the summer holidays came round and he and I set off for Maplethorpe at the beginning of August, as usual. By now, I had steeled myself to disappointment. Ruby had surely had time to have, at least, a look at my manuscript.

It was not until we had been there well over a week that her letter arrived one morning, forwarded on by George. I was quite alone, for Adam was already up at Herbie's hut and Mrs Markby never came on Fridays. I was in the back garden when I heard the click of the latch on the front gate which at this hour usually heralded the arrival of the postman, Archie Turnbull. We never had a lot of mail at Maplethorpe, but somehow I *knew* that today he was bringing me a letter from Ruby. There was the sound of him pushing it through the letter-box and then his feet tramping down the flagstone path again. I did not go to collect it at once. I stood quite still, the garden scissors in one hand, a bunch of red dahlias in the other. Then, summoning all my courage, I walked very slowly into the house, laid the scissors and flowers on the draining-board in the kitchen and went through into the small hall to pick up the long white envelope lying on the mat.

It was still a good five minutes before I could bring myself to open it. I just sat outside on the loggia holding it in my hands. At last, I took a deep breath and extracted the letter that I had so long awaited.

August 8th 1963

Dear Mrs Norbury,

Great-Granny Alice

I am very sorry not to have written to you before about the above. Owing to certain changes of plan I was delayed with my holiday reading and consequently unable to study the material you left with me until a fortnight ago. I was so impressed that I got a colleague to look at it before contacting you. We are both unanimous in saying that it is highly marketable. I can think of several publishers who would jump at it. I can quite understand why you looked so glum about my idea of cutting. It seems obvious that there will have to be two books, i.e. Vol. I and Vol. II.

I also feel that I must apologise for sounding so discouraging when we met. I fear I am automatically apt to do this with new authors. It is always a relief when one can subsequently say unreservedly that they are on to a good thing . . .

I know it was silly, but I sat there crying. I was so *pleased*. My mother had been right. Neither she nor Great-Granny Alice had let me down. How I wished they both could have known. For all I knew, perhaps they did. It would have been so nice. As it was, I felt I simply *had* to tell someone, only I couldn't quite think who. I would, of course, tell Adam when he came back to lunch. And I *could* ring George, but as he was coming down to spend the Saturday night at Maplethorpe, I decided to wait. Besides, although I knew he would react favourably and say all the right things, he couldn't possibly have the same interest in Great-Granny Alice as I did – also it would be impossible for him to understand the *glow*, the feeling of achievement which completely possessed me.

Oddly enough – or perhaps not so oddly – the one person I did want to contact at once was Janet Palmer. In time I would tell Diana Colbert and Prue Tanner, but it was Janet I wanted to speak to, Janet who had worked like a slave getting the manuscript ready for me to take to Ruby Thetford. I got up and went to the telephone.

When I had first visited Janet, she had had her telephone disconnected for economy's sake but I had insisted that it must be re-installed at my expense. She had demurred, but I explained that it would be invaluable if we were going to work on the same project. And indeed it *was*. It saved much time and trouble, for she sometimes had queries – all of them valid – about which I had to give decisions and I myself often found it necessary to ask her to add this and that.

As soon as she heard my news that morning, she was, as I had anticipated, absolutely thrilled. There was something so completely genuine about her 'Oh, *Vicky!*' – I had at last got her to address me by my christian name – and then the way she went on, 'I never dared to say it, but all the time I was typing *Great-Granny Alice*, I kept telling myself, "This is something very special". I just *knew* it would see print.'

'Well, we haven't got a publisher yet,' I said, 'only the verdict of your Ruby and her colleague. But I'm awfully grateful to you for putting me on to her, Janet. I'm sure she's a splendid agent. Now I'll have to get down to work again.'

'Yes. I hope you took a lot of it with you to Maplethorpe.'

'Well, some. But I didn't want to be too optimistic. So far the suitcase has remained unopened.'

'Then you'd better go and open it right now.'

I laughed. The more I got to know Janet, the more I came to appreciate her and understand that perhaps it had not been just a pretty face which had attracted my brother all those many years ago. We spoke a little longer, about Vera, when I might be able to come to Southampton with more typing and the possibility of her fitting in some casual work during August. It occurred to me that perhaps one year I could give Janet and Vera a holiday at Maplethorpe. Then the thought came: How do I explain them to Adam? Should I explain them? And if so, when?

My son came back from a morning's wood-carving with Herbie, well pleased with the result: a small tree-like affair which he announced was for me to hang rings on. 'Or even key-rings,' he said. 'You don't go in much for jewellery, do you, Mum?'

'I suppose not,' I replied, 'but this will really be very useful for those other sorts of rings I'm always losing. We'll stand it in the hall.' I was feeling guilty, because the lunch should have been ready and Adam had caught me deeply immersed in the 1880s. I explained that I had been motivated by my agent's approval of Great-Granny Alice's story so far.

Then my son said something which made that particular morning in August even more special. 'Have you got a copy of the manuscript with you here? I should like to read it.'

15

May 1st, 1880

The poor Queen has had to accept Mr Gladstone as Prime Minister again. Her beloved Dizzy has been beaten by what he himself refers to as 'The Elements – six bad harvests in a row'. It is rumoured that at the PM's first audience with the Queen she was decidedly frosty, allowing him to kiss her hand only with the greatest effort.

On a lighter note I have to report that all the members of my own dear family are well and Lionel has been successful in obtaining a reduction in rent from the Earl, who has also promised to pay the tithe. I have tried to be as economical as possible during these bad times but, on the strength of this news, I decided that I would ask Miss Clutterbuck to make all the girls some white muslin dresses to wear at the fête, as the poor darlings have not had any really new clothes for quite a while. Even dear Miriam, my eldest and who is now naturally filling out, has had to make do with alterations to her old outfits. I got Shiner to take me into Overley in the trap, where I bought the material and several yards of different coloured ribbons to be threaded round the neck and cuffs of each garment and some wide ribbons of the same hue with which to trim their straw boaters. Muslin is so cheap and Miss Clutterbuck so reasonable in her charges. I also took the opportunity of purchasing enough dimity to re-cover two feather mattresses. This is a job which Miss C. can do later on, as there is no urgency. But I would like her to start on the dresses straight away as the fête is to be earlier this year, at the beginning of July. This is a sensible parochial decision as it will come in between haymaking and harvest – honeymoon time as the farming community calls it. Please God the season will prove more profitable now we have entered another decade.

I have been uncertain as to whether to buy some of the cheap frozen Australian lamb now on sale. It seems so disloyal somehow. Besides, it surely cannot be as nourishing. But lamb stew is such a favourite at Ivers and Cook always improves the colour with a few drops of liquid caramel, a tip we got from reading MRS BEETON. *What an amazing housewife she was and, to think, died at the age of only twenty-nine.*

Although, soon after I returned from Maplethorpe, Ruby's predictions about *Great-Granny Alice* proved well founded and she sent me a publisher's contract to sign, I realised how much of a greenhorn I really was in this new world into which I had accidentally stepped. The intricacies attendant on actual publishing and printing as opposed to *writing* were, until now, something I had never thought about. It amazed me that after a book was written there was still, at the very least, a nine months' gestation period – as with a human embryo – before it saw daylight. As for the contract I had been sent, I was completely bewildered. I was asked to promise that I had not submitted anything libellous. Visions of Kate Moon suing suddenly rose to mind. Then there were unintelligible paragraphs concerning rights, percentages, my undertaking to correct the proofs within fourteen days, to give the same publisher *Volume Two* within eighteen months et cetera, et cetera. The list of clauses seemed endless. Thank goodness, I thought, at least I have an agent.

In the end, I decided to write to Ruby and ask for another appointment in which to clear up certain points and possibly sign the contract in her presence. Back came a letter inviting me to lunch with her and an Anthony Webster – a director of the publishing house to which she had sold my manuscript – at a restaurant in Soho in a week's time.

'You've really got the bit between your teeth now, haven't you, old thing,' George said, when I told him.

I smiled. 'Well, it's flattering, I suppose. I just never thought that anything like this would take place.'

I bought a new outfit – a rather well fitting black woollen affair which I happened to find in Richmond – and went up to London to meet Ruby and Anthony on the appointed day, arriving at the rendezvous a little too early. In order not to appear over-anxious, I walked round the block a time or two before plucking up my courage to push open

the swing door. To my relief, they were both waiting for
me in the somewhat murky foyer.

Anthony Webster was a man whom I judged to be
slightly older than I was: good-looking, amusing, full of
optimism, who at once called me Vicky and asked whether
I resembled Great-Granny Alice.

'Heavens no,' I replied. 'She was . . . well, I think you'd
say she was a woman with a very definite *presence*, a rather
unusual character who knew what she was about.'

'And you don't?' He looked at me, one eyebrow raised
above the other, as he stretched out a hand for an olive.

'No,' I replied, my eyes meeting his. 'I am an ignoramus,
especially where this contract is concerned.'

We got on well after that. He actually complimented me
on my own passages, saying that my comparisons between
what he called the 'then and now' were extremely apposite.
I came away delighted with all that had taken place that
day.

When, three weeks later, Anthony wrote to ask if I
would have lunch with him again, this time in a restaurant
in Mayfair, I accepted with alacrity, supposing that there
were further points he wished to discuss.

I was surprised, on arrival, to find that Ruby Thetford
was not to accompany us. However, I settled back quite
happily with the excellent Martini Anthony had recommended and awaited more comments on my manuscript, or possibly some suggestions about the second
volume. It did not occur to me until we were well over
half-way through lunch that we simply hadn't touched on
my writing at all or the various mysterious – at least, to
me – matters connected with bringing *Great-Granny Alice*
before the public.

Now and then, I tried, gently, to steer the conversation
in her direction. I was dying to know, for one thing, what
kind of book jacket Anthony had in mind and eventually
I did manage to bring the subject up, albeit only in a
general kind of way. But my remarks were brushed aside,
literally with a wave of his hand.

'I've never had anything to do with the things, Vicky.
Once a book has gone into production, all that side of it is

left to the experts concerned. My job is simply to suss out and commission a book which I *know* will sell, whatever kind of rubbish it's wrapped up in. And yours, darling, is that kind of book.'

I flushed. The word darling unnerved me, although Anthony did not appear to feel he had said anything untoward. I knew that in his kind of world it was used fairly indiscriminately and that even at Ackerley it often tripped off the tongue of people like Sylvia Pinner. All the same, I wasn't used to being addressed by it myself.

Then, rather to my consternation, I heard Anthony continue, 'If you haven't anything better to do this afternoon, I was wondering if you'd like to come along with me to an art gallery just round the corner in South Audley Street. A friend of mine's got an exhibition on and I promised I'd look in sometime. His stuff's ultra-modern. Not everyone's cup of tea. We needn't stay long.'

'I, well . . .' I looked at my watch. I had actually planned to walk up to Oxford Street and do a little shopping, but it wasn't important and the idea of going to an art show with my *publisher* was certainly a more attractive alternative. I accepted his invitation but mentioned something about being home by six.

He looked at me quizzically. I sensed that he had not only sussed out my book, but me myself, that he knew perfectly well that I did not *have* to be home by six, that by dint of careful questioning throughout lunch he knew far too much about me, whereas I knew hardly anything about him. He had simply mentioned, in passing, that he lived in London during the week, but he did not say where or what he did at weekends or whether he had a wife in the background. I couldn't help wondering if he was in the habit of taking lady authors out to lunch and prolonging such occasions into what surely must be the rest of the afternoon, for it was three thirty before we arrived at the gallery.

Rather to my surprise, I enjoyed the paintings. Prior to my youthful journalistic aspirations, I had had notions of going to art school and I wished I could have concentrated more on his friend's unusual work, without being distracted by Anthony's hand on my arm as he steered me along, making not exactly inaudible derogatory remarks as we stopped before some of the more outlandish exhibits.

We stayed about an hour and then I said, 'Look, I really must go now. Thank you so much. It's been a lovely day.'

'How are you getting back?'

'By train from Waterloo. It's hopeless driving into central London these days. Parking's such a problem.'

'I'll get you a taxi.'

I had been intending to take the tube but, before I knew where I was, we were outside on the pavement and he had hailed a cab. For one alarming moment I thought maybe he was coming to the station with me. Quickly, I put out my hand and he held it fractionally longer than necessary, I thought, as we said goodbye.

In fact, all the way home, I kept thinking about a lot of things which Anthony Webster had said and done that day and why on earth he had *bothered* to take me out in the first place. It was so long since anything like this had happened to me. I was under no illusions about myself. I was coming up forty-three. I was an ordinary wife and mother, who did not try to halt the passage of time as, perhaps, someone such as Sylvia Pinner. I did not go in for facials, hair-dyeing or crash diets. Over the last two rejuvenating measures I was lucky, for I really had no need. I had inherited the Medway family bonus of not going grey and, for some reason, I had so far escaped any tendency to middle-age spread. If I *tried*, as I had that morning, I supposed I didn't look too bad, especially when my hair had been professionaly set and I wore what Great-Granny Alice might have called my *Sunday go-to-meeting clothes* – although my figure-hugging little black number from Richmond would not appear to have much connection with the Sabbath. In fact, it had been rather a daring buy for me, which I had purchased, rather as my great-grandmother had purchased that muslin for her daughters' new dresses, because I, too, had had no new clothes for quite a while and had suddenly felt rich and reckless on the strength of my manuscript's acceptance.

Nevertheless, I was well aware I was no glamour-puss,

not at all the kind of female I would have imagined Anthony Webster would have gone for. That he had obviously taken a good view of me as well as my book was certainly a boost to morale but I cared far more about the latter than the former. As George had rightly said, I had got the bit firmly between my teeth over *Great-Granny Alice* and I resolved to press on as fast as I could with *Volume Two*.

'Good day?' George enquired that evening, when I got back.

'Very.' For some reason I did not mention that Ruby had not been there at lunch and that I had been to an art show with Anthony Webster afterwards.

For almost the first time I could remember, I began to feel sorry for George. By breaking into print, I had broken into a new world in which I knew he would feel like a fish out of water. I was perturbed when, a few weeks later, this state of affairs seemed to be reinforced. For I received an invitation from my publishers with only *Mrs Victoria Norbury* written across the top. It was to celebrate the publication of a new novel by an extremely well known authoress. At the bottom was scrawled, '*Do* come, Vicky, A.'

We were having breakfast when it arrived and I did not show the actual card to George. I lied. I said 'we' had been asked to a publishing party on October 31st. I had no doubt that I could, of course, bring my husband with me.

He put down *The Times*. 'The 31st, Vicky? Can't manage it, I'm afraid. It's the date of the Ackerley AGM.'

16

'It's my belief it all comes from somewhere other.' He was a tall, thin, hatchet-faced man, whose name I did not catch and who had me pinned against a pillar in a room in New Zealand House where the party on October 31st was being held.

'From where?' I shouted.

'How should I know, dear lady,' he shouted back. 'But we writers cannot accept all the credit for our work. Take you, for instance. What did you say your new novel was about?'

'It's not a novel. Nothing like that. It's . . .' It really was awfully difficult to describe *Great-Granny Alice*, in that our writing seemed to have intermingled so much. In the end, I just said, rather lamely, 'I'm only editing something at the moment.'

He appeared to lose interest, although he was kind enough to remark, 'Well, maybe you'll come round to fiction later and if you do, dear lady . . .' Here, his face brightened up again, as he added, 'Remember the stuff will come into your head from somewhere other. You'll be just a cypher, a transmogrifier. You'll be trapped by these damned muses, or whatever they're called. They won't leave you alone once they've singled you out. They say, "Now, look here, Gregory Fawcett" – so *that* was his name, was it – "get this. There'll have to be a train crash in Chapter Thirteen. Work up to it. Kill off Patricia. Be sure to make it a train and not a plane, because you'll need a body, a burial." Hell, the trouble is you'll find you won't *want* to kill off Patricia. She's nice. You're fond of her. But before you know where you are, you'll be crying your eyes out at her funeral service. They're cunning, these muses. They completely possess you.' Suddenly, his eyes seemed to swivel and he roared, 'Ah, Peter. Good to see you, old boy.'

With relief, I allowed my glass to be refilled by a passing waiter and wandered over to the window. We were fifteen floors up and the view was really staggering: a lit-up

London below and a couple of aeroplanes winking their
way over the Thames as they came in to land at Heathrow.
Then I heard Anthony's voice behind me.

'Sorry I couldn't rescue you before, Vicky. I noticed you
being caught by Gregory Fawcett. I bet you heard all about
his theories on creativity.'

I turned and smiled. 'He was quite interesting really,
even if a bit overpowering. I've often suspected that what
writers write doesn't actually come from them, but of
course I'm no novelist, as I told him.'

'But you will be.'

'What *do* you mean?'

'Well, you don't suppose we're going to let you stop at
Alice, do you? Some of your own passages make me think
you certainly ought to have a shot at a novel. Look, darling,
I've got to go and do my stuff but let me take you over and
introduce you to May Tranter, another of our directors.'

He piloted me towards a group in a corner and disappeared into the throng again.

Anthony had asked me weeks ago by telephone if I
would join in a dinner-party his firm was giving later that
evening at the Café Royal. As it was to be a *party*, there
seemed no reason to refuse, particularly as, by the most
incredible stroke of fate, Jill Patterson, one of my girl-
friends who had come to my mother's funeral, had asked
me if I would spend the night with her in Hampstead on
the 31st and then drive to Colchester next day to visit her
daughter – who was also my god-daughter – at boarding-
school. It all fitted in so neatly, it might have been ordained, especially the fact that George would be tied up
with the Ackerley Annual General Meeting and more than
likely to be joining in a large dinner-party himself afterwards.

I bought another new outfit, this time a black moiré
skirt with a high-necked white blouse and a black velvet
waistcoat with gold buttons. It might have been conventional but it was smart and suited me. Even Jill, who has
never been particularly fashion-conscious, remarked as I
left her house that evening, 'My word, Vicky, you really
look the part. Lady authoress out on the town.'

I enjoyed the dinner-party even more than the cocktail one. There were ten of us and I found myself seated between a well-known writer and a bookseller, both of whom were charming and refrained from expounding any pet theories such as Gregory Fawcett had done. At the end of the evening I suppose it was inevitable that Anthony said, 'Wait here, Vicky, after you've got your coat. I'll just say goodbye to the others and then see you back to Hampstead.'

The doorman got us a taxi and, although I was already in it so that I could not quite catch the address Anthony gave the driver, I was aware that it was not that of Jill Patterson. I did not mind. I think I was a little drunk, as much on alcohol as a feeling of success which had been mounting for several hours. I had held my own. I had not felt out of place amongst so many strangers.

Emboldened, I asked, 'Where are you taking me?'

Anthony looked at me in mock surprise. 'Home, Vicky. At least, back to your friend's house. But it so happens I, too, live in her direction and I've got something to show you. Oh, I know. Don't get me wrong. It's not etchings, but it's certainly a work of art which I know you're longing to see. I happened to chance on it quite by accident as I was walking through our production department today.'

I frowned. Then, suddenly, I realised what he was talking about.

'You mean . . . the book jacket?'

'Yes. Not, of course, the finished article. Just a pull. Not even colour yet, although you might prefer it black and white. They'd like your opinion. So I thought: what could be simpler? You can tell me what you think and I can take it back to the office tomorrow.'

I had the strongest experience of *déjà vu*. All this had happened before and somehow Great-Granny Alice *knew* what I was feeling. Once inside Anthony's flat, looking at her picture, she was exactly as I wanted her to be: a proud face with finely-chiselled features, an immaculate coiffure, a little tucker of lace at her throat, staring at me as she sat at her desk, a quill-pen in her hand. Although I had let the publishers have the one and only small sepia photograph of her which I possessed, this rough sketch seemed far more real, far more life-like.

I couldn't stop looking at it. It must have seemed incredibly rude to my host. For several minutes he, his room, even the party I had just come from, were all gone. Great-Granny Alice and I were alone, in collaboration, joint authors although a century divided us.

Presently, remembering my manners, I turned to Anthony, who had evidently been studying my reaction with interest.

'It's *wonderful*,' I said. 'Thank you so much.'

'Don't thank me. Thank the artist.'

'Who is she?' I felt certain that she was female. There was so much women's intuition in the work.

'I don't really know. A young unknown, I believe. Merton, or some such name.'

'Will you find out? I should like to write to her.'

'Of course.' Gently, he took the rough drawing from my hand, put it on the low table before the fireplace, encircled me with his arms and began kissing me.

And, so help me, for a while I let him. I even, for my sins, began responding. It seemed the most natural way in the world to end what had been one of the most memorable days of my life.

But then, I don't know, just when we had sunk down on to a large low sofa, I caught sight of the book cover again. I saw Great-Granny Alice observing my every movement. A still but by no means small voice suddenly said, 'What do you think you are doing?' I sat up.

'What is it, Vicky?'

'I can't. I'm sorry, terribly sorry. I know I shouldn't have . . .' I was still looking at the embryo jacket and he followed my gaze.

He wasn't angry, as he could so well have been. Anthony Webster was a nice man. He simply said, 'I might have known. She has quite a hold over you, doesn't she?'

He got up, went over to a side table and asked me what I would like to drink. I asked for a squash and he had one, too.

We sat talking then, far into the night. He told me a little about his wife, from whom he was parted, that he had an only daughter at a finishing-school in France, of his disillusionment with many things and his sudden hope, on meeting me, that he had at last found a female who was genuine, who never made any pretence at being clever and who was not out to use her charms to promote her writing.

After that night, Anthony Webster became one of my best friends.

17

The Earl's agent called at Ivers this evening about the repairs to the barn. I told him I was expecting Lionel back from Overley at any moment, so I asked Henry Ponsonby if he would care to come in and have a glass of elderberry wine, which he accepted with pleasure. We still have some from a year ago, made according to Mrs Beeton's recipe and stored in a cask Percy obtained for me from his brother-in-law, Arthur Silverthorne. Henry said it was the best he had ever tasted.

I honestly believe the Dewhursts have decided to do every-thing they can to keep their tenants happy because it is so difficult to get new ones, agriculture being in such a sorry state. They sold off two of the outlying farms at Michaelmas and Henry has had to find managers for two others. Naturally, he and I did not touch on such matters.

There was one thing of interest, however, which I did learn. Apparently the Chantry, in the grounds of the Hall, is to become a young ladies' seminary. Hitherto, it has always been earmarked for the eldest son of the family, but no one hears a word about Frank now. His younger brother, Wilfred, at present in the Guards, is to have some special rooms reserved for him at the Hall whenever he wishes to come there. Renting out the Chantry will be economically very advantageous for the Dewhursts and I should think that the place would lend itself nicely to becoming a school.

I immediately thought of the girls. Until now, I have not been dissatisfied with the tuition they have received from Miss Houghton in the village. It has been a convenient arrangement and she has been extremely conscientious. But lately I have sensed that Miriam is becoming restless. She is over-intelligent and I suspect getting a little beyond Miss Houghton's capabili-ties. Besides, old Mrs Houghton is very frail these days and Miriam has told me that on more than one occasion Miss Houghton has asked her to hear the younger ones' recitation, while she herself went to attend to her mother. I should like

Miriam to spend more time on the accomplishments, callisthenics etc., and a little French conversation would not come amiss. Of course, I myself am able to teach the children piano and sewing and even little Hannah is able to make a plain rice pudding, under the watchful eye of Cook. But a young ladies' seminary would provide that extra polish, so necessary when a girl comes out into the grown-up world hoping to attract a husband.

Henry Ponsonby has promised to keep me informed about developments at the Chantry.

I thought of Alice and Henry having their pleasant innocuous *tête-à-tête*. I wondered whether Alice had partaken of some elderberry wine or whether she would have considered it improper to drink alcohol in the presence of a man who was not her husband. It reminded me of my own little session with Anthony some while back, that so easily *might* have been improper but which had turned out in the end to be almost as innocuous.

I had written to thank him for the evening and we had corresponded since in a brief, friendly, informal way. He had sent me the name and address of the artist – Celia Merton – responsible for the cover of *Great-Granny Alice* and she had promised to let me see the original version when completed, as I had intimated I would like to buy it. I was also in touch with Ruby Thetford regarding a photograph of myself and some biographical details – both of which I found somewhat embarrassing to supply – while amongst other matters she wanted to know whether I would like to employ a professional proof-reader. This seemed to me to be a splendid idea. It was therefore arranged that one set of proofs, when they came through, should be sent to a Mrs Dacre, another to Janet Palmer and a third to myself.

I had been feeling a little guilty about Janet, as I had only been to see her once since the summer. Although I had had every intention of pressing on with *Volume Two* as fast as I could, I found I had been slowed up by Christmas and Adam's holidays, when I did not think it fair to shut myself away with my work too much. I was

also concerned about George. He had not been his ebullient
self over the festive season and I wondered whether,
perhaps, he had suspected me of infidelity. But as I had
not been to town since the night of the party – except for
one brief shopping visit, which we had made together – I
dismissed this idea.

Nevertheless, when the better weather came and he still
seemed out of sorts, I suggested – not for the first time –
that he saw our doctor.

As before, he at once became on the defensive. 'There's
no need, Vicky. Best to keep away from such chaps,
especially now old Hardiman's retired. God knows what
his successor will be like. Some young twerp straight out
of medical school. If he can't find anything wrong, as like
as not he'll *invent* something.' He got up and left the room.

But when, a few weeks later, I happened to find George
dosing himself with bicarbonate of soda in the middle of
the morning I refused to let the situation go on any longer
and he allowed me, grudgingly, to make an appointment
for him to see our new GP. On returning from his surgery
the following week George was non-committal, merely
saying that Dr Price wanted him to have a check-up at the
local hospital but he was damned if he was going to do
that. 'If I see anyone else at all, Vicky, I'll do it through
old Kindersley,' he said.

When I pointed out that Sir Derrick Kindersley was not
only retired but a child-specialist, he grew tetchy.

'Don't be a fool, Vicky. I'm well aware of that. But
Kindersley would know all the top brass in the medical
world. You don't suppose I'm going to hang around sitting
on a bench in some draughty out-patients' department, do
you, waiting to see some foreign wallah. I told Price he
could keep his referral form, or whatever it was he was
starting to fill in. Besides, what have we taken out private
medical insurance for, for God's sake? Why don't you get
on with your writing and leave me in peace?'

So I did, but with misgiving. At Easter, Adam brought
Julian to stay for most of the school holidays because his
mother had gone abroad to see his father. Having two
boys was, in many ways, a help. One could let them do

things together which one might not have allowed Adam to do alone. But they had arrived at an age when evening parties were high on their list of priorities and, although there were not quite so many as at Christmastime, George and I found ourselves constantly turning out around midnight to fetch them home. It occurred to me that, as parents, we should be giving one ourselves and that next Christmas I would have to get to work early and arrange one. After all, Ackerley would lend itself well to a teenage party. I felt sure that, because of George, the powers that be would agree to our using the ballroom for this purpose.

But just thinking about an occasion so far ahead made me curiously uneasy. Normally, I could imagine George taking a keen interest in such an affair. Now, I couldn't. He had not mentioned anything to do with health or doctors since his visit to Price and if he had taken any self-prescribed medicine he had been careful not to let me see him doing so. But it was obvious that playing the genial host to his son's friend these holidays was an effort. Many was the day he sent the boys out on the links with the pro, whereas at one time I felt sure he himself would have accompanied them, especially as Adam was at last beginning to show an interest in golf.

I suppose we were both making a valiant effort to pretend that all was well when it most certainly wasn't. As soon as Adam and Julian were back at school, armed with a letter from Dr Price we visited a Harley Street specialist who had, indeed, been recommended by Sir Derrick Kindersley. I think, even before the results of the rigorous in-patient investigation which George was forced to undergo in a London hospital, we knew something was radically wrong, yet we were prepared to deceive each other as well as ourselves. At least, that was how it seemed to me at the time. The doctor in charge of George's case considered an immediate operation necessary to, as he put it, 'remove an obstruction' in the bile duct. He was a smooth relaxed youngish man called Calcott, with eyes that gave nothing away – the opaque kind that I have always found disturbing. I have invariably divided people into those who had good clear 'windows' in their heads and those who hadn't. Mr Calcott definitely hadn't. His eyes were like marbles. Anything might have been going on behind them.

Soon after the operation he had a word with me in private. It was all horribly reminiscent of that which had taken place over my mother, although in George's case I was assured that all was well, that the operation had been a complete success and there was no reason why my husband couldn't go on to lead a perfectly normal life.

'Yet you found . . .?' I began, but was interrupted before I could bring out the fatal word.

'A small obstruction, yes. Very small. Slightly malignant but, as I said, all is well. It has been completely removed. Colonel Norbury should be playing golf again within, say, six weeks.'

'Have you told him this?'

'About the good prognosis? Yes, of course.'

'Did he ask for any other information? I mean, as to the nature of the . . . trouble?'

Mr Calcott frowned. 'Not that I recollect. He just seemed delighted that all was now well.'

George, when I saw him next, was indeed delighted. He seemed almost ecstatic. Calcott, he told me, was a genius. 'And he's a golfing enthusiast, Vicky,' my husband went on. 'I said he would have to join Ackerley. Apparently I'll being playing again in no time. You'd better go back and tell Jack Pinner that I'm reckoning on a round with him the first Sunday in July.' From his bed in a private room of the hospital, George was sitting up, positively exuding confidence in the future.

And who was I to undermine it? I was no doctor. It was, I believed, possible to defeat cancer, especially when caught early enough. But George had delayed quite a time before seeking medical advice, hadn't he? Nevertheless, I kept my fears to myself. And if my husband had his, he was being more than successful in hiding them. Yet, as time went by, I honestly began to think he had none. His faith in Calcott and whatever the man had told him seemed total. He was so transparently relieved. He certainly didn't have those secretive marble eyes of his surgeon.

I supposed, now, we would go on as before, indeed, we *must*; although there were two things looming in the not-so-distant future which bothered me: one was Adam's and my annual visit to Maplethorpe, the other was the publication date of *Great-Granny Alice* at the beginning of September.

I did not want to leave George this year for a whole month. It wasn't right so soon after his operation, even though I knew he would probably try to insist on it. If only he would come to Maplethorpe, I thought, it might do him good; but then I had to accept the fact that it probably wouldn't. He disliked holidays of any sort and I doubted that I would be able to persuade him to take even a short one with me alone before Adam came home.

My second concern was of a much more personal and selfish nature. Ruby Thetford had warned me that there would bound to be a certain amount of razzamatazz at the time of the publication of my book, and it might be as well if I would make myself easily available then for possible interviews et cetera et cetera. To me, it seemed highly unlikely that there would be the slightest interest and, perhaps rather tactlessly, I said as much to her. 'I wouldn't be too sure, Vicky,' she had replied. 'After all, what am I here for? I *am* your agent and your publishers and I are very much behind *Great-Granny Alice*. We intend to do all we can to promote this book.'

I realised that if I was away down in deepest Dorset I could, conceivably, miss out and let them all down. On the other hand, Adam would be bitterly disappointed if *he* had to miss out on Maplethorpe. I seemed to have got myself into a right old muddle.

It was then that I suddenly thought of Janet Palmer and Vera. Would it be out of the question somehow to transport them to Maplethorpe? Would Janet be prepared to look after Adam as well as her daughter in a new environment? It would certainly give the poor woman a change of scene, although hardly the holiday I had once envisaged for them. For a fleeting moment I wondered whether Janet might be prepared to leave Vera in some kind of home, at my expense, for a month. But then I rejected the idea. That

was not Janet's way. But *could* I, *should* I, broach the idea
of both of them going to Maplethorpe, explaining that it
would be much more to my advantage than theirs?

Swiftly following on from this, of course, came the
thought: What would I say to Adam? I would at last have
to explain their existence to my son.

18

'And when did you first think of writing *Great-Granny Alice*, Mrs Norbury?'

The girl perched on the window-seat in my drawing-room at Ackerley looked no more than about eighteen: long fair hair falling like curtains on either side of a pale elfin face. She was wearing one of the shortest mini-skirts I had ever seen.

'I can't remember exactly,' I replied. 'And of course it isn't really I who have written the book. My mother suggested my editing the diaries in the first place and then my great-grandmother just took over.'

'But there is quite a bit of your own writing in it, too,' persisted Miss Le Marchant, who had been sent to interview me and asked to be called Thalia. 'I must say I was fascinated by some of your observations between then and now.'

So she had actually read the book, had she? Done her homework. It was mean of me, but somehow it was more than I had given her credit for.

'Well, yes,' I answered. 'That seemed to come in quite naturally. One can't help comparing what life was like nearly a century ago with what it's like today.' (I had a sudden mental vision of Great-Granny Alice being confronted by Thalia's mini-skirt.) The girl was scribbling furiously now. I couldn't imagine what she was putting down. I wondered if I would be allowed to see it.

'And have you always lived here, Mrs Norbury?' Thalia gave a toss of her head so that the curtains parted and her hair fell back a little. She stared at me intently. In spite of her skimpy apparel, she obviously took her job seriously. I felt that I was not being a particularly rewarding interviewee.

'Let's see now. Getting on for fifteen years, I suppose,' I told her. 'We came here when my husband finally came out of the army some time after the war.'

'Ah, the war. Were you married then?'

'Towards the end of it. My husband was a gunner. I was an AT.'

Thalia looked at me uncertainly. 'An AT?'

'Yes, I'm sorry. How should you know? I was in the ATS. The Auxiliary Territorial Service.'

'Gosh! You mean you were a sort of female soldier.' She regarded me now with awe. Having served in the war seemed to mean far more to her than writing a book. 'Were you bombed?' she enquired, innocently and wide-eyed.

'Well, not exactly. Sometimes one got caught in the tail end of an air-raid when passing through London. But my parents copped it quite badly in my home town of Canterbury especially when the doodlebugs came.'

'Doodlebugs?' Again the look of uncertainty crept in.

'Yes. In 1944 Hitler sent over a whole lot of pilotless rockets. V1s and V2s. Canterbury was somewhat in the front line.'

'How perfectly ghastly. What about your husband? Where was he?'

'Oh, he was out in France. He went over on D-Day. He was with Monty's lot all the time, pressing on to Berlin.'

'I don't know how you stood it.' Thalia was sitting on the edge of the window-seat now. What a miracle it was, I thought, that tights had been invented along with the mini-skirt.

'There wasn't much else to do *but* stand it,' I said, watching her get busy with her pen and note-pad again. I began to feel distinctly uneasy. For all I knew she was saying that Victoria Norbury had been under fire or some damn fool thing like that.

'I'd sooner,' I continued, 'you didn't say too much about the war. I mean, it was all a long time ago.'

'But so, so interesting.' The hair was flicked back once more. Two enormous eyes regarded me, possibly, I thought, as an anachronism.

Thalia Le Marchant found the subject hard to leave alone. George and I gave her lunch in the club dining-room, where she continued to ask questions of us both about those years, while Jack Pinner's eyes strayed constantly towards our table with undisguised interest and admiration.

Round about two o'clock the car in which Thalia had arrived returned and, to my astonishment, its bearded chauffeur got out, produced a large camera and began taking shots of me, George, the portals and grounds of Ackerley and our private apartment. Thalia expressed regret that our son was not available to be photographed and I sent up a silent prayer of thanks that Adam was still at Maplethorpe with Janet and Vera, knowing how much he would have hated the whole proceedings.

His reaction to going there with a strange woman and her invalid daughter – whose identity I was forced to divulge once I knew Janet would undertake the task – was surprisingly matter-of-fact. He was growing up fast. The fact that he had an uncle whom he had never seen who had had some kind of wartime liaison with a woman he had also never seen seemed to affect him hardly at all. He was immensely relieved that he would still be able to spend August near Herbie and the Colberts, particularly as Julian's mother had taken him to the States to join his father. I marvelled that my plan had worked out so well on all sides and that Janet was so thrilled to have such a change.

I had gone down to Maplethorpe for a few days at the beginning to settle them in and had spent another weekend there since. George had raised no objections to my arrangements and I felt that in many ways he was glad to have me at home, even though he maintained he had never felt fitter.

I had to admit that looking at him it was hard to believe he had recently undergone serious surgery and I allowed myself to be lulled into accepting that all was well, that I had misjudged Calcott and that from now on George would be leading a perfectly normal life, just as his surgeon had predicted. With renewed effort I turned my attention to *Volume Two*.

I shall never know just why *Volume One* took off – for that's how I thought of it – in the way it did. After all, Great-Granny Alice was no one important. She was merely the respectable wife of a tenant farmer, quietly doing her duty and bringing up her family in southern England in the latter half of the nineteenth century.

When, after a party to mark the book's publication, rather more important people than Thalia and her chauffeur/photographer appeared at Ackerley to interview me and Ruby telephoned to say that the first impression had sold out and the publishers were reprinting, I found it all difficult to take in.

'Of course, it's Anthony who's been primarily responsible for all this, Vicky,' Ruby said one day over the telephone. 'Once Anthony Webster's really behind a book, as he has been behind this one, I've never known it to fail.'

I kept thinking about her words. I had behaved atrociously. I had almost been unfaithful to George. I had led Anthony on. There was, I knew, a particular name for women who did that sort of thing and then drew back at the final moment. It was a miracle Anthony hadn't taken offence. Instead, he had done all in his power to promote *Great-Granny Alice* and so had Ruby. The week after Adam went back to school I was due to travel north with her for some signing sessions in Midland bookshops. It occurred to me that I should reciprocate in some way and in October I asked her and Anthony down to Ackerley for Sunday lunch, a meal I insisted on preparing myself rather than using the club dining-room.

To my surprise – or perhaps not altogether surprise – everything went remarkably well. George might not be much of a reader but this in no way hampered the conversation. He was, as always, an excellent host and, helped by the fine wine he produced, the occasion became almost hilarious.

But I wished, after they had gone, that I could shake off a feeling of foreboding that was hard to define. It wasn't simply to do with George's illness. I just had a presentiment that, having made capital out of my great-grandmother as well as risking my marriage into the bargain, I was going to have to pay for it in some way. I tried to reason with myself by thinking how much I had to be thankful for: how pleased my mother would have been about the book, that I *had* remained faithful to a very nice man who seemed amazingly fit again, that my son was doing extremely well at school, that I had even managed to give Janet and Vera a so-called holiday and that I was Victoria Norbury with a best-seller to my credit.

George had gone down to the club and, restlessly, I began wandering about, switching on lights and drawing the curtains against the approaching darkness outside. Having now bought the original work for the cover of *Great-Granny Alice*, I had had a new picture-light fitted in the wall where it hung over the fire-place. I paused for a moment in front of it. She was looking at me just as she had looked the very first time I had seen the artist's rough in Anthony's flat.

In spite of the warmth of the room, I shivered as if someone had walked over my grave.

19

Yesterday, while I was sitting at my desk writing this diary, I looked up to see a strange creature going by the window. There was a mist rising in the water-meadows, so I only caught a vague glimpse of her, but she was dressed most unconventionally, her skirt well above her ankles and her hair also seemed to be short and curling about her face, instead of neatly swept back into a bun or chignon. At first, I thought she must be a child, but then I felt she was of middle age – although she passed so quickly it was difficult to tell. As there was no knock at the door, I imagined she had taken the wrong turning and gone on down to the village through the farmyard. It is possible she was a guest of the Dewhursts. Lady Dewhurst is keen on the arts and is apt to entertain writers and musicians and painters from time to time. We in the neighbourhood naturally never see much of them, but I believe that occasionally one or two have taken it upon themselves to go for a walk, as the lady I had just witnessed in her peculiar and, I cannot help thinking, rather fast garb. Miss Clutterbuck mentioned to Cook that it was thought Miss Ellen Terry stayed at the Hall last week, but I am certain the apparition hurrying past my window was not the beautiful, talented and always immaculately attired Miss Terry.

It was the word 'apparition' which got me. I had just finished writing out the invitations for Adam's Christmas party and had turned to the diaries with a sense of relief. Although the deadline for the completion of *Volume Two* was constantly in my mind, I found my work, once I got down to it, ever more absorbing. There was so much I had learnt, so much I had yet to learn. But never before had an entry brought me up short, as it were, like this one.

Then I chided myself: Don't be a fool, Vicky. You're letting your imagination run away with you. You're tired. You've been trying to fit in too much lately: a second book-signing in the west country, a visit to Janet, plans for the holidays and Adam's party, keeping a watch – as unobtrusively as possible – on George, and trying not to let more than a day or two go by without working at *Great-Granny Alice, Volume Two*. Why shouldn't she have seen some odd character going by her window?

Yes, but why did she bother to write about it? I mean, as whoever it was didn't actually *call* at Ivers, what possible interest could there be in this woman, a woman dressed, seemingly, not exactly in accordance with the times? Besides, it was misty. On her own admission, Alice hadn't seen her well. Surely my great-grandmother had more important things to record.

There was nothing else about this female until a few days later, when I read:

I keep thinking about our visitor that never was. It was the way she was dressed. I suppose I might have taken her for a gipsy, but for the fact that, although curious, she looked in no way unkempt. Lionel was out pigeon-shooting up at Ivers Copse at the time, but I asked Cook and the other servants whether they had seen anybody. I thought Cook gave me a funny look. She shook her head, but said she would ask Miss Clutterbuck next time she came whether she had any idea as to who it might have been. I don't altogether approve of Cook being so friendly with Miss C. and I said I would ask her myself, which I shall do next Tuesday.

I simply couldn't wait to read next Tuesday's entry. Great-Granny Alice didn't write every day, but I was fairly sure she would put down something as soon as she had spoken to Miss Clutterbuck. I skipped through a short paragraph after the rector's sermon on Sunday. Then, as soon as I began reading *Tuesday, October 18th, 1881* I began to feel quite cold. I stared at the page in disbelief:

Miss Clutterbuck says that some time ago, when she was renewing the chrysanthemums on her mother's grave, she saw a person such as I described going into the church. It was morning, but the wintry sun was low in the sky and when she looked up she was a little blinded by it. There had been rain in the night and some of the white marble tombstones were glistening in a remarkable way. She was struck by the unusual apparel the visitor seemed to be wearing. Miss C. felt it must be a visitor, for she had never seen anyone like her in the village. But when she got home Miss C. wondered if she had been mistaken, perhaps deceived by a trick of light. However, not long afterwards she thought she saw the same figure standing outside Widow Shergold's cottage with something that looked like a kind of notebook in her hand. The odd thing was that this time Miss C. distinctly remembered Percy going by and touching his forelock, although this person did not respond in any way. I suppose, not being one of the village, she mightn't, but I do think it is very important to be courteous at all times to the lower orders. I have tried to instil into the girls the necessity of setting an example, that manners maketh man – and woman . . .

I was shaking now. A feeling of total unreality – disembodiment, if you like – took hold of me, as if there were no time or, if there were, it had stretched, like a concertina, so that Great-Granny Alice was at one end and I at the other. I could see her writing those words with the aid of an oil lamp and here was I reading them in the glare of a 100-watt bulb. Somewhere in between lay the darkness of years, a murky tenuous link between two spotlights.

I did not hear George come into the room. Only when he said, 'Good God, Vicky, what the hell's the matter? You look as if you'd seen a ghost,' did I manage to make some sort of answer.

'I don't know,' I said. 'I guess I'm not feeling too bright.'

'Well, you certainly look as if you could do with a drink.' He went over to the side table and poured me a stiff whisky. It was just what was needed. George is good, more than good, at knowing what to do in any given situation except, of course, that I was not sure what kind of situation this was, any more than he.

'You're not going down with anything, are you, old girl?' he asked.

'It's possible, I suppose,' I lied. I couldn't tell my husband that I had been reading – or thought I had been reading – about my own ghost. It was all too far-fetched. He really *would* think I had gone off my head or had a high fever, if nothing else. Hitherto, I had always rather prided myself on being sensible, dependable, not given to fanciful ideas.

'I've thought for some time,' he remarked, watching me a little too closely for comfort, 'that maybe you've taken on a bit too much, letting your publishers pin you down to a date for *Volume Two*. It doesn't *have* to be in their hands by April, does it?'

'I can't fall down on a contract,' I replied. The whisky was beginning to take effect. I was prepared to believe I was just a silly ageing woman, probably going through the Change, as Great-Granny Alice might have assumed.

Then, to my astonishment, George said, 'After Christmas, when Adam's back at school, why don't you and I really get away? I don't mean to the ski-slopes like Jack and Sylvia Pinner, but how about a trip to Madeira? By boat. I know you don't care for flying.'

Just at that moment I was prepared to agree to anything. I was so grateful. I had a husband in a million. How could I ever have come near to being unfaithful to him was incomprehensible. *Of course* we would go to Madeira when Adam went back for the spring term. For once, I could break my routine and let the diaries go hang. In fact, after what I had just read, I wasn't sure I ever wanted to see them again, although I knew I would have to.

Christmas came and went. Julian Wainwright stayed with us for Adam's party, as well as both the Colbert children. It was, I think, a success, although not something I would want to undertake too often. I realised that in a year or so's time many of the young men present would have probably passed their driving-tests, that even now Adam had asked for the cup we were serving to be 'gingered up with some kind of alcohol'. The responsibility for caring for the younger generation weighed heavily with me. I wished we were back at the shorts-and-tricycle stage. I wanted time to stand still.

Time. Whenever I thought about it, the entries in Great-

Granny Alice's diaries about the stranger at Ivers came instantly into my mind. I wondered whether I would simply omit them in my edited version. After all, it was I who chose what should or should not be published. It was impossible to reproduce everything. The book would then run into far more than two volumes, more like ten. Mine was the say-so, as it were, and this business of the oddly clad visitor had no real bearing on Great-Granny Alice's life. Or had it? She had mentioned Ellen Terry and the Dewhursts, and Miss Clutterbuck being a little too friendly with Cook. That alone, irrespective of whatever it suggested to me, presented a graphic and rather telling little vignette. And what if the mystery were later solved? But it wouldn't be. Of that, I felt sure.

It was when George and I were out in Madeira at the end of January and I honestly began to feel that this total break from the diaries would send me home full of renewed enthusiasm for finishing *Volume Two*, that I found myself becoming concerned about them all over again. Although perhaps 'concerned' was not the right word. In many ways, meeting Professor Avery gave me a lot of food for thought, which was not entirely unwelcome.

George, ever gregarious, had already got to know him in the bar before I met him a few nights later. After dinner he came over to where we were sitting, saying he understood from my husband that I was the author of *Great-Granny Alice*, which he had read with much enjoyment and interest.

I made one of my usual deprecatory remarks about being pleased, except that I was not exactly the author, at which Professor Avery said, 'No? But the book would hardly have seen print without you, would it? I think you have done a service, especially to students of history.'

'A service?' I believe I must have looked at him quite blankly.

'Yes. By contrasting two separate eras in the way you have, you have brought them to life in the most remarkable way. Your great-grandmother and you can certainly put things across. When do we expect *Volume Two*?'

'I'm meant to deliver it by April and then, well, it's at

least nine months after that before it comes out, isn't it? But I'm sure you know much more about this than I.' I was aware that he was a professor of history with countless books to his credit, although I seemed to remember reading somewhere in the press that he had been vilified for holding certain unorthodox views to the detriment of his hitherto rather distinguished but pragmatic career.

He smiled. 'Most publications of mine take far too long to write and far too long to print. It's the sense of immediacy that I have appreciated in your work. The human touch, if you like. Let's hope your publishers make an exception and bring out Number Two before next Christmas. I shall watch out for it. You should have big sales.'

I couldn't help feeling flattered. Here was this man of letters giving me all these gratuitous compliments. The three of us sat talking about this and that for quite a while and then, the following day, he came and singled me out on the verandah when George had walked down into Funchal to buy another film for his camera.

'I wanted to ask you something last night,' he began, 'but I sensed that you did not want to talk too much about *Great-Granny Alice*. However, I'm leaving tomorrow and I hope you will not mind my enquiring whether you experienced any problems with time in connection with your work?'

'Time?' The same cold uneasy feeling that I had begun to know well started creeping over me once again. 'How do you mean?' I hedged.

'Well, it's rather my hobby-horse, I'm afraid. You see, if one throws oneself into the past, as you obviously have, don't you occasionally find it difficult to get back into the present? You must sometimes have thought you were actually *at* Ivers with your great-grandmother.'

I was thankful that he was not looking directly at me, but staring out to sea. I hoped he had not noticed that I was trembling.

'Yes,' I said, at length. 'Yes, I do find it difficult to, well . . . hop about. To travel, as it were.' And then, all of a rush, I found myself adding, rather stupidly, I felt, 'Goodness knows by what method.'

He turned to me and smiled. 'Method? You're not thinking of ordinary forms of transport, are you? Have you never heard of the ladder of time? People get on and off it at will. It's a delightful experience. I mean, if I find my work's getting me down, I don't always come away to Madeira. I can simply relax for an hour or two in a little holiday taken not in life as we know it today, but in *time*. I leave, not England for foreign parts but, say, 1860 or any other year I fancy. I don't choose a period I have been working on as a historian. That would be no holiday. But I take up some book which presents the past accurately yet vividly, just as yours did. That was why I was so taken with it. Sometimes I have lived with Aubrey's *Lives* or Pepy's *Diary* or Boswell or gossiping Creevey. In a moment I am transported into another world, where I can enjoy my surroundings and my fellow men without obligation or anxiety.'

For several minutes there was silence between us. I was vaguely aware of the blueness of the sky, the sea, some boats, the diminutive figure of George walking slowly up the hill towards us. The scene was a travel agent's dream, one which Great-Granny Alice would never have seen. Or would she? If it were possible to go back, presumably one could go forward. What about all those people who had presentiments, who dreamt of things to come: H.G. Wells and Priestley, for instance?

'We'll crack it one day,' I heard my companion continue, 'this business of time. Not in this millennium, maybe.' When I still remained silent he said, 'To get back to more mundane matters. I wonder . . . if ever you happen to be Oxford way, would you care to have lunch with me? Or perhaps London would be more convenient?' He brought out his notecase, extracted a card and handed it over.

'Thank you,' I said. 'Thank you very much indeed. I would certainly like that. Meanwhile, you've given me such a lot to think about. I really am most awfully grateful.'

And I was. I did not think I would mind going back to whatever the rest of Great-Granny Alice's diaries had in store for me.

20

It would be wrong to say that after George and I returned from Madeira I skimped my work on the diaries. If anything, I went at them more intensely, but I certainly felt I had to hurry. April seemed such a short time away and I had decided I would have to write some sort of concluding chapter in an effort to bring the curtain down.

Apart from my initial visits to Ivers, I had subsequently only made much briefer calls, usually *en route* to somewhere else. Now, I knew a somewhat longer spell was needed if I were to capture the present atmosphere and, if possible, get it across in my final pages. Prue had constantly asked me to stay at the house again and, although at this point I felt reluctant to do so, I thought I would try to forget about my fears and take her up on her open invitation. After all, I had read nothing else about Alice's strange visitor, although my conversations with Professor Avery were often in my mind. When *Volume Two* was published I intended to send him a copy and maybe also take *him* up on his open invitation to lunch.

It had occurred to me that an alternative to staying at Ivers would have been to see if I could put up at *The Plough and Sickle* with Kate Moon and her son and daughter-in-law. But then I realised that not only was this a cowardly way out, but that Prue would be mortally offended.

So, towards the end of February, I found myself going off to spend another weekend under Great-Granny Alice's roof. I had not quite finished reading the diaries, but I had got through almost a decade. I had learned of Percy's marriage to a daughter of one of the gardeners at the Hall, his move to the smallest cottage on Ivers farm – as well as the whole of the Dewhurst estate – the birth of two of his children, and my great-grandmother's fears as to what would happen when the predictable others came along: *heads to tail and all in the same bed, I suppose*, she wrote, *unless a switch with our old dairyman and his wife can be arranged, now that their family has fled the nest*.

Thanks to another graphic piece of writing, I had been

able to visualise in detail Miriam's marriage to the eldest son of Henry Ponsonby in 1884, a union which appeared to find much favour in her parents' eyes. My great-grandmother had made a special point of mentioning – just as she had when describing her own mother's funeral – that: *the Earl and Countess of Dewhurst sat immediately behind us in the church*. Latterly, there had been references to Alice's feeling a little *indisposed*, to Lionel suffering from gout and how he had at last given way to her insistence that the girls should all be inoculated against small-pox, a measure he had hitherto strongly mistrusted.

Many national events were interwoven with domestic ones: the death of General Gordon, the arrival of the first motor-car, the right of most men to vote, the completion of the Canadian-Pacific Railway and the Queen's coming Golden Jubilee. All of these fell somehow quite naturally between Great-Granny Alice's accounts of her own charity work, some cryptic comments on the Poor Law and the pleasure the whole family derived from her reading *Black Beauty* and *Treasure Island* aloud every evening.

It should have been a hotch-potch, but it wasn't. The entries were alive, convincing and beautifully observed. I felt grateful to have been privy to this vanished world and knew that, in spite of Professor Avery's kind remarks, my own writing fell far short of my great-grandmother's artistry. It was this that was sending me to Ivers again. I was so anxious to produce a good ending to my work, however much I might have preferred, at this stage, not to go.

It was dark when I arrived on the Friday evening, but an outside light in the porch shone out a bright welcome as I drove up the lane. Prue came to the door at once, surrounded by all her children, explaining that her husband was hoping to be back in time for dinner on Saturday night, a meal to which she had also invited Alaric. In the midst of so much admirable domesticity, I wondered how I could ever have felt anything remotely supernatural had taken place at Ivers. It now seemed just what it must have been in my great-grandmother's time: a typical solid happy family home: walking-sticks in the front hall, wellingtons in the back, even an up-to-date edition of *Mrs Beeton* in the kitchen.

I had been put in a south-facing bedroom with a window looking towards the village and the church. Prue informed me that her daughters had picked and arranged the vase of winter jasmine and early polyanthus placed by my bed, for which I hoped I showed due appreciation before handing over the presents I had brought for them: books for the two older ones, pencils and paints for Caroline and a rather superb publication that had just come out on English country gardens, which I thought their parents might like.

Once the children were in bed, Prue produced a delicious meal for us both, which we ate in the dining-area of her kitchen. Her present *au pair* had apparently gone into Overley for the evening. My hostess started regaling me with all the local news and then began apologising, saying that such mundane matters could hardly be what I wanted to hear.

'On the contrary,' I replied. 'It's *just* what I've come to hear. To wind up *Volume Two* I want, if I can, to portray Ivers and the surrounding district as it really is today. You're giving me the *exact* information I was hoping for and why I'm afraid I'm battening on your kind hospitality again.'

'Oh, good.' Her face lit up. She was an extraordinarily attractive and generous woman. 'Tomorrow we'll go walkabout. Take you to see the institutionalised Hall, the Chantry School which has come under new management and is, or will be, educating all my daughters. I do *hope* the weather's fine.'

It was. It was one of those warm sparkling early spring days which I remembered my father saying always came at least once each February. His 'February Day', he used to call it. Accompanied by the children, we even walked up the right of way across the lower slopes of Hackpen Hill to Ivers Copse. After climbing the stile there, we had to pass through a patch of undergrowth which I was informed was known as the Wild Wood because of the Tanner family's attachment to *The Wind in the Willows*. The two older girls raced ahead, but I could quite understand why Caroline hung back and placed a small hand in mine.

Once out in the open again we had a superb panoramic view of this little bit of England in which, like that around Maplethorpe, I felt I had some kind of stake. I looked down towards Ivers, lying there so peacefully in the spring sunshine. I thought of Great-Granny Alice going about her business, her children who had gone to the Chantry School when it had first started. I thought of Percy, hungry and poorly shod, rook-scaring on Hackpen Hill on Christmas Day, and my great-grandmother's valiant efforts to improve his lot and that of his mother, the Widow Shergold. Because there was now only a faint tracery of green showing on the trees, it was just possible to discern her cottage down by the mill. It was all there, all I had read about, all I had taken it upon myself to reveal to a wider public. I turned to Prue.

'Thank you so very much,' I said, 'for bringing me up here this afternoon.' I wished I had spent more time at Ivers instead of running away from it.

The dinner-party that evening rounded off a marvellous day. I felt it would have been good to have had George with me. Prue had, indeed, asked him, but I think he felt that Ivers was very much my scene and, of course, the countryside had never held much attraction for him, especially at this time of the year.

I slept soundly for the second night running and on the Sunday morning we all went to church, Caroline being taken out by the *au pair* before Alaric's sermon. I was pleased to see that he had quite a fair-sized congregation; and I was also pleased to feel that Prue was bringing up her family in just the way of which Great-Granny Alice would have approved. She would surely have been delighted with the modern occupants of Ivers.

I hadn't been to church, other than at Christmas or Easter and Adam's confirmation, for years and felt that I had fallen down badly on my son's upbringing in this respect. He and I had gone to matins and stayed on for communion last Christmas but, subsequently, other more worldly pursuits had taken precedence every Sunday before he went back to school. I wondered whether it was now too late to make amends in the forthcoming holidays.

It was a remark made by Caroline at lunch that suddenly shattered my sense of well-being and tranquillity and broke the train of thought which had been forming in my mind as to how to tackle my last chapter. With a spoonful of lemon soufflé half-way to her mouth, Prue's youngest daughter piped up, 'You wore a hat last time you came to church.'

I also paused with my spoon in exactly the same position.

Prue smiled and looked at Caroline indulgently. 'Mrs Vicky,' – as I was nicknamed by the family – 'hasn't been to church with us before, darling. You must be thinking of someone else,' she said.

'No, I'm not,' the voice replied, emphatic, affronted and absolutely sure of itself. 'It was a fur one.'

I was aware that they were all looking at me now and also that I had begun to tremble. I *did* have a fur hat and also a cloak, which I had bought in one of my rare fits of extravagance soon after *Volume One* had come out. I recalled wearing them both when Adam and I had gone to our local church last Christmas. During the service Ivers had been much in my mind. It was almost as if I could *see* Great-Granny Alice and her family sitting in one of the front pews in that other little Norman church at Compton Ivers. This hadn't struck me as odd at the time. I knew that, being so involved in the past, I was, as it were, 'tuned in', so that my senses were heightened, my memory sharpened. I had often made jokes about having a kind of television screen inside my head, especially when I was writing. It was rather a help then, although not quite such a help when it came to everyday life. Any visitor I was expecting had only to be a few minutes late and I could picture them under a bus or lying in a ditch. Imagination, out of control, was the very devil.

All this flitted through my mind as I struggled to say something normal and reassuring to Caroline. In the end, I felt I made a poor job of it. I desperately wanted to put the child at ease, not make her feel she had said anything silly. 'I think I often look like other people,' I told her. 'Lots of them have faces like mine. And fur hats.'

Caroline stared at me, unconvinced. Her lower lip stuck out, just as Adam's used to do when he was thwarted as a little boy. She remained silent and I think we were all rather glad to let the subject drop.

I could have been mistaken about what happened when I was leaving. They all came out on to the front drive to wish me goodbye, Caroline by now her usual smiling little self, saying, like the others, 'Come again. Please come again soon.' I started the car engine. It was when I was almost on the point of moving forward that she poked her head in the window and whispered something I couldn't quite catch.

Had she, I wondered all the way home, tried to tell me that what she had said at lunch was a *joke*? Or had she said something about my also having worn a *cloak*?

21

I find it hard to write these words. Harry, my poor brother, has met with a fatal accident and I feel so responsible for it. Last Thursday, he rode over to see me. I fear he was in debt to the bookmakers again and wanted the loan of twenty pounds.

I was feeling poorly that day – although I must not excuse myself on such grounds – but my stomach was certainly troubling me; and, of course, Harry's requests for money have become more numerous and for increasingly large amounts of late. I have tried to keep all this from Lionel but, on my brother's previous visit, my husband came into the house unexpectedly and found out what was happening. Lionel himself is not averse to gambling. After all, he likes nothing better than a game of Farmer's Glory with friends, but he does not approve of betting on the horses, particularly of farmers who go to the races during harvest. He did his best to forbid my helping Harry out any more. He really got beside himself, saying that I must let my brother go to the devil in his own way.

So this time I told Harry I was sorry but I could not lend him any more money – also that it was not lending but giving, as he never paid me back. It was Harry who then got beside himself, swearing and going very red in the face. (I have long thought his doctor ought to get the leeches on to him to let some blood.) He stormed out of Ivers and went to The Plough and Sickle. He is said to have left there about ten o'clock, the worse for drink. Rumour hath it that his horse has more than once had to find his own way home, carrying an inebriated master.

That night the poor animal must have stumbled or Harry was too drunk to keep in the saddle. Percy came across his body as he rounded Dead Man's Corner when he was walking up to the dairy at four o'clock for the next morning's milking. (It's odd how unlucky that particular spot has always been. It didn't acquire its name for nothing, by all accounts.) Percy told Cook that the funny thing was that he could have sworn there was

*a woman bending over Harry when he first spotted him. Of
course, it was still dark, there was only a fitful moon and he
really only had the light of his lantern to go by. Besides, it was
windy and, as like as not, there were probably plenty of moving
shadows from the trees overhead. Anyway, by the time he
turned round to see Harry's horse grazing nearby and then
back again to the body, whoever or whatever he thought he
saw had disappeared, so he felt he could have been mistaken.
Certainly, no woman has come forward and poor Percy has to
give evidence at the Inquest.*

*I couldn't help thinking about the time when I saw that oddly
dressed woman going by the window at Ivers, but I must not
let myself become prey to imaginings. There are quite enough
fanciful females in the village at present. Miss Clutterbuck is
definitely going through the Change and so is Miss Houghton.
I am relieved to have all that behind me, although I do not
understand why I am so troubled by indigestion . . .*

I wished, how I wished, I had not read that entry. I was
so near the end of my task and now I was once more
overcome with the weirdness of it all. I could think of no
other word. Any good which the holiday in Madeira,
or talking to Professor Avery, might have done, seemed
entirely negated.

I wondered, not for the first time, if I had worked by
another more conventional method – simply arranged and
read the diaries straight through, as probably any professional historian would have done before putting pen
to paper or even going to Ivers – whether things might
have been very different. I would have noted Great-
Granny Alice's references to her 'visitor' as an interesting
phenomenon, nothing more. By becoming so *involved*
as I went along I was constantly committing myself to
two separate centuries, my spirit in one, my body in the
other.

Then, with an effort, I took myself to task. I was talking
– or, rather, thinking – nonsense. As Alice had wisely
remarked, one must not give way to *imaginings*. Little
Caroline Tanner had obviously tried to tell me that what
she had said at lunch had been a *joke*; and there was no

doubt a perfectly rational explanation for the unknown visitor who had occasionally been seen at Ivers. Besides, country people, especially in those days, were well known to make a bit of a story out of the most flimsy evidence. There was no wireless or television to divert them, so they made up for that by tending to see things in their minds, rather as I did when writing. Rumour and superstition proliferated. Down at *The Plough and Sickle* the daily lives of local inhabitants would have been greatly enhanced by some really good tale about a ghost or a witch, its perpetrator always able to count on being stood an extra pint or two for providing them with some welcome entertainment.

I worked on, although with effort. Sadly, I found my great-grandmother's writing deteriorated both in quality and quantity as illness sapped her strength. There was the briefest account of Lionel taking Hannah to the continent, to which my mother had once referred. How much this brevity was due to Alice's physical condition or how much to genuine embarrassment at her husband's unfortunate lapse in having lost at roulette and wiring for money to get home, I would never know now. My mother had really only given me the bare bones of the story and Great-Granny Alice had by no means embellished it. I wondered just how much she was suffering at the time. I was sure that her valiant spirit would have seen that she kept it to herself which was why, I supposed, Lionel had not realised sooner that something was seriously amiss. I also wondered how it was that he had evidently been able to pass off his own irresponsible behaviour in the light of his reaction to his brother-in-law's peccadilloes. There was no word of condemnation from his wife in the relevant entry, merely regret that her dear youngest daughter had not seen Italy. Among Alice's countless other virtues was utter loyalty to her spouse.

It seemed sad that I had no one to turn to for any extra information which I might have been able to pick up; for my grandmother, Hannah, had been the only one of Alice's children to continue the line. Miriam had died without issue and of the three other girls, two never married and the third died of puerperal fever after giving birth to a still-born son nine months after marrying a neighbouring gentleman farmer.

With a shock I realised that Adam was now Great-Granny Alice's sole descendant and if anything happened to him the Medway line would be quite wiped out. Yet why on earth had I thought about that? It was morbid. Why should anything happen to Adam? In all probability he would marry and perhaps have several children who, in due course, might even reap a little benefit from the royalties of my two books, should they remain in print.

Thinking of Adam reminded me that George and I were due to pay him a visit at school the following Sunday. That was always a great pleasure, something to look forward to. I had a sudden fierce desire to get away from the diaries, to get back to life as it was before I ever started working on them, to ordinariness, even to the rather boring banal daily round at Ackerley. I wasn't an author; what I had done was a fluke. I might have let success temporarily go to my head, but I wasn't going to let that happen any more.

It was painful reading Great-Granny Alice's last entries, to learn of her faith in recovery, yet her increasing dependence on Dr Allingham, senna pods and, towards the end, morphine. *It certainly eases the colic wonderfully*, she wrote,

and please God in the New Year I shall have taken a turn for the better. I am now adhering to a strict regime: I rest on the day-bed both morning and afternoon. I eat no red meat and Cook has been instructed to put all my vegetables through a sieve. I do believe that this is helping me. Dr Allingham is so good and attentive. I cannot think what we should do without him. He has become a real friend of the family. The other evening he stayed on to have a glass of whisky with Lionel in the drawing-room. It was quite a while before I heard him go out and greet his groom, who was standing by with the trap.

What, I wondered, had the doctor said to Lionel? Surely he must have warned him, over that drink, of the serious-ness of his wife's condition? It seemed plain to me that my

mother had been quite right in her surmise that she and
her grandmother had suffered from the same disease, the
only difference being that in Alice's day diagnosis would
have been far more difficult: no X-rays and the opening
up of the colon unheard of.

It was an entry right towards the end of the diaries,
made only a few weeks before she died, that was ever to
stay in my mind. My great-grandmother was patently
sedated. She could even have been wandering. Her writing
was extremely faint and at first I could make no sense of
what I read. I thought she was referring to the Queen, for
I managed to decipher *Victoria* and then the words: *will do
it.* Or I *thought* that is what they were. There followed four
almost indecipherable lines, but the last one brought me
up short. The feeling I had begun to know well started
creeping over me again as I began to pick out: *She is so
interested in Ivers . . . I like to think of her reading. . . .* The
writing went faint once more. To whom was Alice referring? Surely she wasn't imagining she had been writing
for her beloved Monarch? On the other hand, maybe the
morphine had produced an euphoria or a distorted sense
of her own importance, something from which, when in
good health, she had never suffered, albeit there was no
doubt she had a wholesome and proper pride in herself
and her family.

Besides feeling shaky, I also felt cheated. I wanted the
mystery cleared up and now it never would be. It seemed as
if I could look at it in whatever way I chose. Great-Granny
Alice's last thoughts had gone down to the grave with her
and dead men – or, as in this case, dead women – tell no
tales.

Or do they? I went in search of a magnifying glass and
studied the entry again. It was definitely *Victoria* she was
on about and, on closer scrutiny, I found she had written:
will have a good idea of the place by now. . . . The Queen,
surely, wouldn't have had any idea about Ivers. But *I* had.
I had only to close my eyes and there it was, thrown up
on my private mental television screen. I recalled the day
I had stood by the copse looking down on it, with Prue
and her children. Was it too much to hope that perhaps in

a hundred years' time one of my descendants might do the same? That he or she, having read *Great-Granny Alice*, was interested enough to want to make a personal visit? But how different would it be then? What changes would have taken place? Good grief, a motorway or some such other invention might have altered the area out all recognition. Annihilated Ivers. Wiped the village of Compton Ivers off the face of the map. But unless some ghastly new conurbation had sprung up, at least the contours of the land would remain, wouldn't they? Land was everlasting, wasn't it? And what about the river? One couldn't easily deflect the course of a river. I hoped the one I knew would still flow along through the twenty-first century, just as it had done since time immemorial.

I suppose I was guilty of wishful-thinking. I must remember how speeded up life had become. We had put a man on the moon, we had made the atom bomb and God alone knew what else the human race might get up to. Thinking about God made me think about life after death. Until I started editing the diaries, I don't think I believed in it. Now, I wasn't so sure. I suddenly recalled how a mistress at my school had once said that life was like a river. When one was living it one couldn't see what was coming round the next bend. But if one was up in an aeroplane one could see the past, the present and the future all at once. When I died, might my spirit be up there somewhere, looking down, off the ladder of time, as Professor Avery had intimated? It would be good to talk to him again. I promised myself that I would get in touch with him as soon as *Volume Two* was out of my hands. There must be *something* beyond one's understanding. If there were not, what was life all about? Why, for instance, had my great-grandmother bothered to record her own? Why was I, Victoria Norbury, possessed of her priceless diaries, now stacked away neatly in an old chest belonging to my mother? And what had prompted *her* to ask me to edit them?

I went to bed that night perturbed, puzzled, unable to sleep.

'What's the matter, old girl?' George asked, when I got

up in search of a couple of Disprins. 'Bugged by old Alice again?'

'Yes,' I answered. 'I suppose that's a very fair way of putting it.'

22

It was the last week of April. I sat in Anthony Webster's office, the second Volume of *Great-Granny Alice* lying on the desk between us. He smiled at me. His eyes had that same amused, kind, welcoming sort of look in them which I remembered well, although he seemed older, as if the past few months had not been easy ones.

'Congratulations, Vicky. Most authors never complete to a deadline.'

'Don't they? I hate letting anyone down.'

'Yes, I know.'

'Of course, this mightn't come up to expectations. You could be disappointed.'

'Hardly, I think. Not if you've gone on drawing those very pertinent comparisons. Did you come up against any snags with the second half?'

I hesitated. 'Not exactly.'

'How do you mean?'

'Well, I couldn't help getting rather more wrapped up in the time factor, wondering which century I was in. I suppose . . . I occasionally let my imagination run away with me.'

'Which is why I'm so keen on your writing a novel for us.'

'Oh, Anthony, . . . I don't think I . . .'

He held up a warning hand. 'Not *now*. Have a break. Just bear it in the back of your mind. Do something else for a while until, as I'm sure that chap Gregory Fawcett warned you, it'll all come tumbling into your head from somewhere other.'

I laughed. Yet, if I were honest with myself, I knew that half of me wanted to accept the challenge, even though the other half was scared stiff. But it was cheering to feel that someone thought I *could* write a novel and also that no one in the literary world ever quite pooh-poohed the idea of muses, or the subconscious, or simply that there were more things in heaven and earth. . . . On the other hand, I wasn't prepared to go any deeper with Anthony into the exact snags I had encountered over the second volume of *Great-Granny Alice*. With the book, hopefully, on its way to the printers, perhaps they would be exorcised.

'I wish,' he continued, 'you'd let me give you lunch. Are you *sure* you can't get out of this other engagement?'

I shook my head. 'No, it's awfully kind of you, but it's . . . well, I'm meeting someone who enjoyed the first volume, Professor Avery.'

'*Avery*? The historian?'

'Yes.'

'Well, well, Vicky. You certainly do pick them. I wonder . . . do you think we might get him to review *Volume Two*?'

'Oh, *no*?' I became alarmed. The last thing I wanted was for the Professor to feel I was using him in any way. 'I met him in Madeira,' I said. 'I was interested in his theories on Time, that's all. He suggested meeting again and as he's coming up to the Athenaeum for a few days, I promised to lunch with him there today.'

'I see. You know, I suppose, that he occasionally brings out a book under a pseudonym?'

'No, I didn't know.'

'Well, I think he reckons, quite rightly, that his somewhat way-out theories might jeopardise his reputation with regard to his widely acclaimed more scholarly works. He's highly thought of in the academic world. I believe he's a very interesting man. However, if I can't give you lunch today, I hope you'll let me do so . . .' and here a certain mischievousness crept into his manner, 'when we get a pull of the jacket. I remember it meant a lot to you last time. Have you got any ideas as to what you'd like to see on *Volume Two*?'

I shook my head again. 'No. That young artist did such a marvellous job on Number One. I'd sooner leave it entirely to her.'

'Good. That's a deal, then. I'll ring you as soon as she comes up with something and we'll have that lunch.'

We said goodbye and I made my way to the Athenaeum, where Professor Avery was waiting for me in the Ladies' Annexe. I was struck by how distinguished he looked as he rose to greet me: a tall thin white-haired man with deep penetrating grey eyes, today formally dressed as opposed to the more casual clothes I recalled him wearing in Madeira. Now, he looked every inch the learned professor, with his dark suit, bow tie and bulging briefcase beside his chair.

After we were seated and he had ordered two dry sherries, he reiterated, as he had done in his letter, how delighted he was that I finished what he referred to as, 'Your compulsively readable and worthwhile task.' Oddly enough, he then went on to enquire, just as Anthony had done, whether I had come up against any difficulties in bringing about its conclusion.

As before, I hesitated. How much could I, should I, tell him about my fears and fancies? He might think me mad. Yet he had certainly hinted at things not altogether of this world when we had last met. I tried to recall exactly what he had said. I believed that, in all probability, he would be sympathetic.

Suddenly, I found myself saying, 'Sometimes I couldn't help feeling that what I was doing was . . . well, ordained. I suppose it sounds quite ridiculous but I wondered whether my great-grandmother knew about me. I can't really explain it. Often, I seemed to be with her – or she with me.'

He nodded. I thought how strange it was that here was this eminent professor of history, who had written I don't know how many erudite tomes – including what was considered to be the most authoritative work on the Industrial Revolution ever produced – not looking in the least surprised at the remarks of a comparative tyro who had had the temerity to suggest that she had experienced something inexplicable compared to any rational thought.

'Ever since I read your first volume,' he said, 'I was aware of the intensity of your rapport with your great-grandmother. I suspect this probably increased with *Volume Two*. That is why I asked if you had come up against . . . difficulties.'

I stared at him. His perceptiveness was uncanny. I began, then, to tell him about Alice's 'visitor'. We became so engrossed in conversation that a waiter had to come and remind us that our table had been booked for one fifteen.

'Have you,' Frederick Avery asked during the course of the meal – we were by now on christian name terms – 'read any books on this sort of thing? J. W. Dunne's *Experiment With Time*, for instance? Or Einstein's theories on time and space?'

I had to confess that I hadn't

'You should,' he continued. 'Many people believe that all Time is always there, happening at once: the past, the present and the future. After all, if you think about it, why should there be so many instances of *déjà vu*? Or individuals having some kind of presentiment about things which actually come to pass, if those things weren't already happening? I suppose I first became interested in such matters as a young man because I had a cousin who suffered from *petit mal*. Now, don't get me wrong. He was in no way mentally impaired. He was a highly intelligent individual who went on to do brilliantly in the scientific world. But he told me that sometimes when, say, he might be playing bridge, he was aware that part of his brain would cut out, that he was witnessing a whole century or centuries, living some long historical saga in a split second. No one at the card-table ever noticed anything amiss. He was still able to make a perfectly rational bid.'

I listened, fascinated. We seemed to be alone, for the other guests had departed. The waiter who had urged us to lunch now returned to urge us back into the small foyer, where he brought coffee.

'My cousin wasn't the only person I knew who got me thinking about Time. When I was an undergraduate at Christ Church, I went to stay with a friend whose mother had written a county history. She seemed a very normal down-to-earth sort of person, but she told me one night at dinner that some five years previously when she had first been working on the book, she had driven to a remote village at the foot of the Pennines, where some archaeological dig was reported to be in progress. Unfortunately, she was held up and did not reach her destination until evening was closing in. She was distressed to find a mist rising, no sign of the 'dig', but there appeared to be a fair in progress. For some little while, she sat in her car watching the scene, which was lit by flares and torches from the booths and side-shows. Every so often some rather primitive swing-boats flew in and out of this circle of light, where coconuts rolled from the sticks on which they had been placed and bottles were shivered by gun-shots and fell to the ground. She remembered being sur-prised when one of the swing-boats suddenly failed to return into the lighted area.'

I sat there listening to Frederick Avery. I felt I could have sat on all night. If anyone could tell a good story, it was he. He seemed to warm to his theme, no longer the pedantic professor.

'Just before I went to stay with my friend,' he continued, 'his mother had been working on updating her original manuscript. She explained, that night at dinner, how quickly a book of this kind becomes out of date. To assist her, she had been glancing through one of the short new guide books, the sort used by tour operators, just to check that there was not some vital change in the county which she might have overlooked. She was surprised to find a reference to this particular village, saying that there had always been a fair held there, until it was abolished in 1850 due to a mishap connected with one of the swing-boats. She tried to think back to the fair she had witnessed and what the people had been wearing, but her memory could not come up with anything other than nondescript brown garments, the sort of clothes adopted by country people anywhere and at almost any time. But she was so intrigued – besides being a stickler for *facts* – that she had written to the present rector of the village to enquire whether, by any chance, some isolated fair had been held there five years previously. That very morning she had received a reply to the effect that he could categorically state that no such fair had taken place during his long incumbency of forty-five years.'

'So she had, in fact, seen a ghost fair?' I hazarded.

'Yes. You can quite see how this sort of thing aroused my interest. I could have made it my life's work, although

I was aware, even at that young age, that it might be financially rather a risky subject on which to base any future career.'

It was getting on for four o'clock. Reluctantly, I stood up. Before standing also, Frederick Avery leant down and extracted a book from his brief-case. Then he handed it to me, with diffidence. It was entitled *The Timeless Moment* by A. R. Thornton. On the front cover was a picture of a clock, but with no hands.

'One of my sidelines,' he remarked, 'although, strangely enough, it's now turning out to be more lucrative than some of my histories.'

'Thank you,' I said. 'Thank you so very much. I can hardly wait to read it.'

He smiled. 'When you have,' he replied, 'perhaps we could meet again.'

23

To one who has ever been acutely aware of the transience of life,
I read in the train going home,

> *who has tried, however inadequately, to study the passing of*
> *generations, to look upon the past, present and future as one*
> *and indivisible and Time itself as immeasurable, it would seem*
> *that the artificial clock which man has invented to help him*
> *through the brief spell he spends on this earth, is merely*
> *something which begins to tick against him at the hour of his*
> *birth and ceases when his eyelids close in death. In eternity he*
> *will have no need for such an apparatus.*

When I arrived at Ackerley, *The Timeless Moment* had me
completely captivated.

'Good day?' George enquired.

'Very. And you? How did your appointment with
Hetherington go? New glasses?' Because George had been
having a little difficulty reading small print lately, I had
urged him to see our local oculist.

My husband did not reply at once. Then he said, 'Hetherington wants me to see someone at Moorfields.'

'*Moorfields*?' I was instantly on the alert. What did that
mean? Did George have a cataract? Or a detached retina?
But wasn't he rather on the young side for that sort of
thing? Perhaps not. After all, he was coming up fifty-six.

'When?' I asked, rather lamely.

'He got his secretary to ring through. I'm to see a chap
called Frith next Monday. It's probably nothing. Hetherington's always struck me as a fuss-pot, a bit of an old
woman. While we were waiting for the appointment to be
fixed up he told me he does *petit point* in his spare time.'

'But didn't he *say* what he thought might be wrong?'

'No. Just that he detected a little abnormality at the back
of the right eye. He thought it best if I saw Frith at the
hospital, where they have every facility for doing further
tests.'

'Oh, I see.' Yet I didn't see, at least I only saw that

something was much more wrong than George was letting on. The very fact that the appointment with a specialist had been made so quickly was proof of this.

I wanted to accompany my husband to Moorfields, but he insisted on going alone. 'It'll mean a lot of hanging about, most likely, Vicky. Whatever's the point of your kicking your heels in some waiting-room?' He had always been a man to dislike fuss.

I said goodbye to him on the Monday with misgiving. The hours seemed to drag interminably. Having given the second volume of *Great-Granny Alice* to Anthony, I was at a loose end, feeling as bereft as on those days when I had seen Adam off to boarding-school. At midday I did something I very seldom did when alone. I went down to the club and allowed Jack and Sylvia Pinner to persuade me to have a drink with them. Immediately, I began regretting it. I knew George did not want any mention of the reason for his absence and Sylvia would keep making idiotic arch remarks about him going off to see *his* publisher, having got his own back on me by writing a book entitled *Confessions of a Club Secretary*. Not for the first time did I wonder just how Jack managed to put up with her.

It was well past seven when George got back. In the space of ten hours he appeared to have aged twenty years. I found myself looking at an old man, as well as a frightened one, however much he tried to hide this. I believe I knew then that he did not have long to live. I kept thinking of something I had read in *The Timeless Moment* which now didn't make sense. *It seems in the long run*, Frederick Avery had written, *of comparatively little account whether a man falls in battle in youth or dies in old or middle age. He dies so soon, in any case.* . . . But it *did* matter, surely, to those who are left. If ever I saw the Professor again, I would take him up on that.

'I had a brain scan,' George said, flatly. 'They want to operate.'

He poured us both a stiff whisky. Then he continued, 'You might as well know, old girl, I've thought for some time something wasn't quite right up top. I suppose the bloody canker's broken out again. Pretty vile place it's chosen to do it.'

'But George, Calcott said after your gall-bladder op that you were clear . . .'

'Of course he *said* that, Vicky. But did you *really* believe I was taken in by all that claptrap? I think you should give me credit for having had a bit more brain at that time than what I'm likely to have from now on.'

I wanted to go over and kiss him, hold him, but I held back. Ours had never been that kind of relationship and yet, what *could* I do to help my husband of over twenty years, who now went on, 'I was pretty awful, I know, old girl, over your Ma's last illness. But I've had a horror of the wretched disease ever since I was a child.'

I noticed that George still did not actually use the word cancer. Then, to my surprise, he added, 'Ever thought about those wild roses in the hedgerows, the ones that turn into great green bulbous things? My nursemaid used to say they were diseased, had canker, in fact. I believe that started my fear. Possibly it's why I've never been all that keen on the countryside.'

I saw now, in a flash, something I should have seen years ago. I might have some kind of second sight or hindsight or whatever it was in connection with Great-Granny Alice, but I was woefully lacking in understanding my own husband. This time I did get up and go over to him and we sat there just holding hands for a long while.

The authorities wasted no time. George was to enter a clinic specialising in eye and brain surgery the following Sunday night. Jack Pinner was going to take charge of Ackerley in his absence and had promised not to divulge the exact nature of his illness to anyone, especially Sylvia. Without being as much as actually untruthful, we had allowed it to get around that George was being operated on for a cataract. I had arranged to drive him to London on the Sunday afternoon and had booked myself a room at the ex-service women's club, where I had once given Janet lunch. The management had kindly allowed me to reserve it for an unspecified length of time, according to how things went.

On the Sunday morning, having packed for us both, I went down to the garage at Ackerley to take my car along to the local petrol station. I was surprised to find that George's car was not in its usual bay beside mine because, by a kind of tacit understanding, he had not driven at all since he had been to see Frith. I supposed that, as it was such a short journey to the pump, he had possibly decided to have his own car filled up, although I could not quite understand why. When I arrived at the garage, thinking I might pass George *en route*, I was alarmed when the attendant told me that 'the Colonel' had indeed called in about half an hour previously and then left with a full tank heading towards our nearest town.

It was then that the dream which I had had the previous night came back to me. It had been worrying me ever since I had woken up that I could not remember it, because it had seemed important. Suddenly, I saw the scene as clearly as if it were happening at this very minute. There was George's hospital room and a doctor and nurse standing by his bed. The doctor was holding a watch and murmuring, 'He should have been here by now.' I knew then that I would not be driving George to London for his operation.

Looking back, I think it was inevitable that as soon as I reached home I went straight to an old chest where he kept his relics of the last war: his uniform, medals, a manual or two, programmes of several West-End shows we had seen together – and his revolver, for which he conscientiously renewed a firearm certificate on the appropriate date. The chest was kept locked, especially because of Adam when he was small. Today it was not. Even before I began searching, I knew that the gun would be missing.

The police, when I telephoned, were swift, efficient and kind. I gave them George's car number and in no time at all an officer, together with a policewoman, arrived. After further questioning, the latter stayed with me throughout the rest of the day.

It was an incredibly beautiful one. I sat in our window-seat and looked out over the Surrey landscape, watching the sun going down behind blue-green hills, seeing a foursome walking back from the last tee: small puppet-like figures having engaged in a pleasant innocuous pastime on the Sabbath day, men who would probably be off to work on the morrow, making money for their wives and families, fixing up another game mid-week. It was all so normal, so ordinary. Why had I knocked Ackerley so? And my husband's role in it? He had been providing a service and a very good one. People needed such relaxation, such companionship. I was overcome by remorse. My mother had known a thing or two when she had said that men needed more than catering for. I might have known that George would decide not to go through with the operation. Bad enough to have a tumour on the brain, doubly bad to come round from an anaesthetic after its removal, possibly turned into a cabbage or an idiot. Silently, I saluted my husband for his bravery.

I think the young policewoman must have found me curiously detached and calm about the present situation. I simply sat on, thinking about George's and my life together, while the shadows lengthened and darkened and finally merged with the night. The telephone did not ring and I did not suggest ringing the station. The news would come through in due course. When, at midnight, it did and she told me that George's body had been found beside his car at the edge of Ashdown Forest, I thanked her and asked to be left alone.

'But . . . will you be all right, Mrs Norbury?'

'Yes,' I replied. 'I shall be quite all right, thank you.'

I remained in the window-seat for the rest of the night, trying to work out how best to tell Adam.

24

An inspector came with the note the following day. It had been found on the front passenger seat of George's car, carefully held in place beneath a guide book.

Dearest Vicky,

I pray you will forgive and understand. Knowing your infinite compassion, I believe you will. But to me, this way out seemed the best for us all. I hope you will be able to get Adam to see that. Even if I came round from the operation relatively unscathed – and the chances of that, I discovered, were considered less than 50/50 – the THING would only break out again within a limited time. I thought it better to make a simple quick exit when I was fully capable of doing so.

I think you will find my affairs pretty well in order. The authorities at the club will, I am sure, let you stay on until you've found somewhere else to live which is to your liking. I fancy you may want to make a bid for Maplethorpe. Even though the owners have not previously wanted to sell, they might consider a really good offer. With what I have left you and your own recent not inconsiderable earnings – so well-deserved and over which I have much admired your diligence – you should be in a position to do this. Adam, of course, will soon be leaving school and needing help and guidance over his career. Your mother's trust fund will be of great assistance here. If he is determined to go in for woodwork – as seems to be the case – that college, Sandalheath Manor, which you once went to see, would seem the best bet. I know I have been against the idea and I still cannot think he will ever make much money at it, but at least he has never wavered in his aims. Most youngsters haven't a clue what they want to do. I believe, indeed I am sure, he will be the greatest comfort and support to you . . .

There then followed explicit details and instructions concerning his solicitor – with whom he had lodged his Will – his accountant and a request that no one but the former should attend the briefest form of cremation service. This, at first, I found hard to accept, until I realised that maybe, because George was intending to take his own life, he felt it more appropriate that neither Adam nor I should attend his funeral. In the event, we complied with his last typical and strangely endearing proposal, for, after sending us both his love, he had written, *Why don't you just take Adam out from school that day and go and have a picnic.*

So that is what we did. By then, I had begun to feel doubly grateful for my husband's thoughtfulness because, owing to the fact that George had made his reasons and intentions so palpably clear, the inquest was simply a formality at which my presence was not required either.

We went, on Adam's suggestion, up on to an old turn-pike, where you could just see the sea in the distance and there didn't appear to be a dwelling in sight. The English countryside spread out all around us in the sunlight, bright and green and full of promise at that time of the year. Some words of poetry kept trying to form in my mind. For a while I could not quite remember them or think where I had read them. Then, in a sudden flash, they came back to me. I realised that I had not read them in any book, but on a stone – a memorial stone erected on similar downland to the memory of their author, the Wessex poet, Richard Jefferies: *It is eternity now. I am in the midst of it. It is about me in the sunshine.*

It was a long time before either of us spoke. My son lay on his back, staring at the sky. Then he said, 'Do you believe in an after-life, Mum?'

I did not hesitate. I *could* not hesitate, not now, with so much evidence all around me. 'Yes,' I replied, simply. 'Yes, I do.'

We lapsed into silence again. A sparrowhawk hovered somewhere above us. A small animal made a rustling noise in the bushes by the side of the track. There was a faint scent in the air, common to all such places: a mingling of wild thyme, gorse and bracken. I felt as if I were caught up in something inexplicable, lost in, or, rather, a part of my surroundings, so that the grass on which I was sitting was as alive as myself. Silently, I thanked George all over again for taking care of Adam and me so well that day.

When I dropped my son back at school in the evening, he said, 'It'll be nice if you do buy Maplethorpe, Mum. You will, won't you? And if I go to Sandalheath Manor I won't be too far away. I'll be able to get home most weekends, I hope.'

It did not escape me that he had already referred to Maplethorpe as 'home'.

I managed to buy it that autumn, even though George's solicitor and accountant, as well as the agent I employed, told me I was paying far too much for the place. Indeed, they all did their best to dissuade me, but I remained determined. Adam wanted it, I wanted and, after all, had not my husband himself given his blessing to the project.

In many ways, the fact that I had booked to rent the place for August as usual, made the final move both easier and more difficult. It was easier because, once I knew Maplethorpe was to be mine, I could start planning accordingly with a local architect for future alterations. It was difficult because I was needed at Ackerley to deal with the handover to the new young secretary and his wife, Jack Pinner being by no means qualified, willing or even the right age to step into George's shoes on a permanent basis. Once again, I fell back for help on Janet Palmer who, although she had Vera to care for, came to Maplethorpe and proved herself invaluable, especially as the proofs of *Great-Granny Alice, Volume Two* suddenly arrived on the scene. In between all Janet's domestic duties, besides coping with multifarious unexpected problems which kept arising, she sat diligently checking them thrice over.

Oddly enough, I found leaving Ackerley more of a wrench than I would have thought possible. When saying goodbye to Jack and Sylvia Pinner I found myself extending a genuinely heartfelt invitation to them to visit me at my new home, an invitation which was taken up with equal enthusiasm.

For I realised that Ackerley, despite all its limitations, had been a permanent and secure base for practically the whole of my married life, the place where I had reared Adam, produced *Great-Granny Alice* and where I had known, come what may – apart from a few brief months prior to my mother's death – the unfailing support and affection of a loyal husband. As I watched two removal men take down the picture of my great-grandmother from above the fireplace, I was smitten – as so many times of late – by remorse at my own shortcomings. There was so much I had taken for granted. George, dear George, had possessed that other unfailing quality of always being *there*. Now, I was setting out alone. In the very nature of things, I could not, must not, expect my son to be with me for more than limited periods each year, even though I was becoming more and more aware of how right George had been in saying that Adam would prove to be the greatest comfort to me.

Fortunately, that winter, there seemed so much to do that I did not have time to brood too much, and the constant proximity of the Colbert family was the greatest boon. Just as Frederick Avery had hoped, *Volume Two* of *Great-Granny Alice* was due to appear a little before Christmas and Ruby Thetford had already been on to me regarding advance publicity. But what with everything which had happened since I had delivered the manuscript into Anthony's hands, I was no longer keen to enter into the razzamatazz which I remembered had surrounded the publication of *Volume One*. I had, moreover, all but forgotten my odd experiences while working on the diaries or, at least, they had been conveniently relegated to the back of my mind – that is, until a morning in mid-October when Archie Turnbull pushed a typewritten letter through my letter-box with my publishers' insignia on the back. *You must have been wondering what on earth has happened about the jacket design for* Volume Two, wrote Anthony,

We're terribly late with it, I'm afraid, but Celia Merton has been ill. Knowing how taken you were with her first effort, I decided to risk waiting for her to come up with the second. She tells me it is now in the post, thanks be. Remembering that 'date' we agreed on back in April, I thought how nice it would be if you could get up to town either later this week or early next, when I could show you Celia's rough and give you lunch. I do apologise, Vicky, for springing this on you. I could, of

course, send a photostat, but it would be so GOOD to see you.
I do hope Maplethorpe is coming up to all expectations . . .

Normally, I would have jumped at Anthony's suggestion.
Anything to do with *Great-Granny Alice* had always had
my full attention. But somehow, George's death, the move,
arranging for Adam's entry to Sandalheath Manor after his
A-levels the following year, had altered my priorities.
Travelling to London – now so many more miles away –
seemed less and less attractive. So I rang Anthony who,
though disappointed, was understanding and kindly
agreed to send me a copy of the jacket design as soon as
it came to hand.

I don't quite know what I was expecting. I had such
confidence in the artist and was only too glad to feel
she had been given an entirely free hand. When Archie
Turnbull knocked on the front door of Maplethorpe two
days later, because he couldn't get the large stiff envelope
through the letter-box, I simply took it from him with
pleasurable anticipation. Only when I was back in the
kitchen opening it to reveal the back view of Great-Granny
Alice seated at her desk staring out of the window, past
which a shadowy figure was hurrying along in a kind of
swirling mist, did I catch my breath and have to sit down.
It was so uncannily true to the scene which I realised I had
always had in my mind's eye. The passing figure was so
very like mine. I realised that Celia Merton knew what I
looked like, for we had met when I agreed to buy her first
original; but why, out of the whole book, had she chosen to
portray Alice's apparition? And had she, without knowing
anything about those odd experiences I had had, unconsciously used me as a model, thus turning the 'visitor' and
myself into one?

It seemed to me that this particular entry in the diaries
must have impressed itself on her as much as it had on
me, even more than the similarly curious one concerning
the lady who, according to Percy, had been bending over
poor Harry in the fitful moonlight. That would surely have
made a more arresting picture. But then I realised from the
selling point of view it was probably imperative still to

have Great-Granny Alice on the cover of the book; and even though it was just her back view this time, it was superbly done: the erect sitting posture, the immaculate coiffure with a shining bun in the nape of her neck, the desk so neatly appointed, the ink-stand, the quill pen, part of the diary peeping out on the left-hand side, the dim outline of a grandfather clock in the background to the right of the picture.

It was only when I was in bed that night, having given Anthony an enthusiastic go-ahead on the telephone, that I switched on the light to take one more look at the cover for *Volume Two*. It did not really matter and I certainly did not propose to query it for, after all, the clock was obviously meant to be more of an impression than anything else. All the same, it reminded me of the cover of another book I had been given earlier in the year. In keeping with *The Timeless Moment*, this clock had no hands either.

25

I suppose, of all the curious incidents of which I had been so aware while working on my great-grandmother's diaries, Celia Merton's rough for the cover of *Volume Two* affected me the most.

I kept staring at it in the days following its arrival – since it was a photostat there had been no need to return it to Anthony – and the more I studied it the more I realised how good it was. I did not for one moment regret having given it my wholehearted approval, although I still felt my resemblance to the figure passing Alice's window was horribly uncanny. On the other hand, I kept reminding myself that Anthony had not remarked on this. Was I, perhaps, reading or seeing things into Celia's drawing that really weren't there? Had I, in fact, been doing this sort of thing for the past several years?

Looking back, when I thought carefully about the various occurrences which had troubled me, I could come up with perfectly rational explanations – or near enough. I could put my fears down to an over-active imagination, coincidence, an obsession with my task upon which George had more than once remarked. I seemed to remember reading something somewhere about 'emotional attachment to a cause impeding objective assessment'. Yet, this recent development had really struck home.

Although I had still to see the finished version, I was as eager as before to purchase it on completion and I rang Celia Merton to this effect, while at the same time offering her my sincerest congratulations. From our one and only meeting, I recalled her as a quiet, rather reserved person, but I could tell on the telephone that she was pleased that *I* was once more pleased with her latest achievement. Encouraged by this, I decided to start a little questioning: what, for instance, had made her choose Alice and the 'visitor' as a jacket illustration? There was such a long silence that I felt I must have overstepped the mark, committed some offence against the artistic temperament by asking for an explanation which she either could not or would not give. Then, just when the pause was beginning to get embarrassing, I heard her say, 'I simply thought it interesting. I wondered who it was that your great-grandmother had actually seen.'

It was on the tip of my tongue to reply, 'But didn't you think it was me? You've made her *look* like me.'

But I held back. Celia obviously hadn't thought that or surely she would have said so. Faced with her somewhat equivocal answer, I certainly wasn't going to refer to the clock. She could easily take a comment on its lack of hands as some kind of adverse criticism. Then and there, I resolved that I would, at least, never talk about the similarity to anyone – at least, not unless anyone first mentioned it to me.

'Black and white and shades of grey like last time?' Celia said, before we rang off. 'It doesn't seem to be a subject which lends itself to colour.'

'Oh, *yes*,' I answered. 'It couldn't be anything else, especially with . . . well, the scene outside the window.'

Shades of grey, I thought, as I put down the receiver. So apt. The expression seemed to fit so many aspects of my work on the diaries, especially on those events which I had found most puzzling. I could interpret them as I wished: areas of dark mysterious sinister grey or pale, almost light-hearted airy-fairy ones. Much better to think of them as the latter. If *Volume Two* had what I considered to be an impression of me on the front, so what. My photograph on the back flap above the 'biographical details', which Ruby Thetford had managed to elicit from me, showed a very different kind of woman: an ordinary mousy middle-aged housewife, not at all like the wild-eyed indistinct creature dressed in what seemed to be a loose flowing garment – I could not help noticing that it might or might not have been a *cloak* – hurrying past the windows at Ivers in a swirling mist. No wonder Celia Merton had not connected the two of us.

There was little I could do now regarding the book's publication, except wait. I had promised to undertake a signing session, but this was to be in a local bookshop not far from Pennyford. The publicity people seemed anxious to make a kind of feature about my new whereabouts, but I had declined to be interviewed again. For one thing, Maplethorpe was in the usual mess caused by building alterations, but the real reason was that I did not want anyone like Thalia Le Marchant coming down to ask me the reasons for my move. It had been a genuine support and comfort to receive the condolences of people like Anthony and Ruby and Frederick, but the idea of having to discuss my bereavement with comparative strangers was utterly unacceptable. I found myself missing George constantly, longing to refer to him whenever some problem cropped up, sometimes even forgetting that he was not there to be asked and that it was only I who could fall back on my limited knowledge or maybe burrow amongst some old files for an answer.

Often, I wondered what he would think about my plans for Maplethorpe. Would he approve my idea of turning the outhouse into a kind of separate little flat for Adam, with a bathroom and a kitchenette and a bedroom on a raised platform at one end of the largish sitting-cum-work-room? Was I being extravagant in creating another bathroom in the house itself and installing central-heating throughout?

'Gosh, Vicky, you're really going to town, aren't you,' Diana Colbert said one day, when she caught me poring over catalogues to do with spiral staircases and radiators and stoves. 'You're turning Maplethorpe into a dream-home.'

I suppose I was – or trying to. And yet, that night in bed, I began to wonder who and what for. I had no husband. Nor was I likely to marry again. Adam, in time, would probably marry and I would be left growing older, rattling around in Maplethorpe doing what? Since George's death, I realised I had been so relieved in having something to throw myself into – especially with his blessing and the diaries out of the way – that I had allowed my dream-home to become my *raison d'être*. But now, I had a sudden panic as to how I would occupy my time when all the improvements were finished.

It was just then that I received another letter from

Anthony, asking if he might call in on his way to Cornwall. Apparently there was some recluse who lived near Truro who had at last agreed to see him in connection with one of his ancestors' essays which Anthony wanted to reprint. As the man never came to London, Anthony had decided that the only thing to do was to drive to Cornwall. *It will be a rotten journey at this time of year*, the letter ran, *but the thought of seeing you and Maplethorpe will make it so very much more worthwhile.*

So I gave Anthony lunch one raw November day a week later. I was sorry about the weather and the fact that the house was still upside down, but although he showed great interest in what I was doing to it, during the meal he gave me one of those quizzical looks I remembered well and put me immediately on the alert.

'I do have one other reason for breaking into your new rustic domesticity, Vicky, apart from the pleasure of seeing you.'

I knew, then, what was coming, but I did not exactly help him.

'*Great-Granny Alice*, God rest her soul, is, or soon will be, off our hands. Apart from the efforts being made by Ruby Thetford and our publicity department to get her well received, she'll be launched on the world at large. I often think that seeing a book come out is a bit like seeing a child leaving the nest. You've probably thought that yourself. One can only hope and pray. Of course, in Alice's case, she's already been *accepted*. The public liked her and are eager for more of her company. What we all want to know is whether her perpetrator will now think about writing something else.' He became suddenly hesitant, as if wondering whether he might be upsetting me. Then he went on, quickly, 'I don't want to pressurise you, Vicky. You've had a wretched time. But well, perhaps when you've got Maplethorpe to your liking, do you think you might consider that novel after all?'

'But, Anthony . . .' I started to make all the protestations I had done before, and yet, far from upsetting me, I still found it flattering being actually *asked* to write a novel. It was good to feel that someone did not think I was a one-book or, rather, a two-volume author. And had I not myself been worrying about how I was going to fill in my time in the future?

Sensing that he was on surer ground, Anthony continued, 'The thing is, we don't want to let you fade from public view. Oh, I know that sounds dreadful, but if someone has an imagination like yours and can write into the bargain, it seems a criminal waste not to put that to good use. You *will* give it some thought, won't you, Vicky? Maplethorpe seems just the place for the muse to strike. It's almost Hardy country, isn't it? Or even Lorna Doone. I'd so like to be able to go back to London and think of you sitting at that desk of yours in this delightful setting working on . . . well, I leave that to you. Sadly, publishers have no imagination. Otherwise, they wouldn't remain publishers.'

I laughed. He extracted a promise from me that I would at least think about his proposal and we chatted about this and that for the rest of the afternoon. I asked him about his mission to Cornwall and he told me that his firm was bringing out a collection of essays on folklore and he was anxious to include one on Lyonesse, which some people declared was an ancient town lying sunk beneath the sea off the coast near Land's End. This man's ancestor claimed to have seen it.

'*Seen* it?' I asked. 'But how long ago . . . ?'

'Well, he couldn't have, really. But, you know, Cornwall is full of such individuals and alive with superstition. And Lyonesse *is* the ancient name for the county. There's more than one person who swears they have seen a jumble of towers and domes and spires and battlements out at sea. It must be some sort of mirage, a trick of light and then susceptible types perpetuate the story, embellish it, so to speak.'

'But do *you* believe it?'

'Oh, Vicky. I find it awfully hard. But it's a subject which seems to fascinate people. Holds their attention. I've told you, I'm just a *publisher*. I want to publish books that will sell. That doesn't mean I'm knocking imagination. Look what I've just asked you.'

I thought of the mother of Professor Avery's friend who had seen a ghost fair. I thought of my own unusual experiences. I wanted to ask Anthony if he had noticed the similarity between myself and Alice's visitor on Celia's cover picture. But somehow I couldn't. Not after what he had just said. And I had vowed that I would never bring the subject up, not unless someone else such as Frederick Avery gave me a lead. And it was so manifestly plain that the thought had never crossed Anthony's mind. Soon afterwards, with reluctance, he got up to go.

On parting, he kissed me on both cheeks. Ours was quite a different relationship now. Almost, one might say, cosy. After he had gone, I thought back to the publication of *Volume One*, of my euphoria, naïveté, excitement at entering another world and how I had been seduced – or almost – by both it and Anthony Webster, until Celia Merton's book-jacket, thank God, had put paid to that.

Involuntarily, I looked up at Great-Granny Alice's picture. Although Maplethorpe was still in turmoil, I had managed to have it hung above the sitting-room fireplace, just as it had been at Ackerley. I know it was silly, but if I stared hard enough, I could have sworn today she was looking down at me quite approvingly.

26

Dearest Vicky,
I can't thank you enough for **Great-Granny Alice, Volume**
Two. *I've read it from cover to cover – ENGROSSED! Even*
the hectic business of Christmas didn't stop me. It was a super
present and all your separate ones to the children were so much
appreciated. You will be receiving their individual letters in a
few days – I hope! Peter is now half-way through the new
volume and is as absorbed in it as I was, so you'll probably be
getting another letter from him, too. We feel we have such a
personal stake in it. Perhaps 'stake' isn't quite the right word,
but you know what I mean. I'm so glad to think we were here
and could help in however small a way, especially as I'm afraid
I now have some rather sad news.

We are leaving Ivers, Vicky! Peter's father died quite unex-
pectedly out in Australia just before Christmas. He was the
head of the family firm. I don't think I've ever told you much
about it, but it's quite an important real-estate concern in
which a lot of relations have shares. Peter was the only son and
he feels it's up to him to go back and take care of things,
particularly for the sake of his mother and sisters. And, of
course, as I expect you realise, airline pilots are always retired
early. It will be the most appalling wrench for me and the
children, but I've sometimes wondered if this might happen one
day.

So – it's possible our dear Ivers may be advertised in Country
Life *shortly. Peter would like to leave by the end of March. You*
simply MUST come before then. PLEASE,PLEASE,PLEASE.
I've no idea who our successors might be, but rest assured that
I shall do my level best not to sell it to anyone who I don't
think will cherish it. I've so loved living here and to have had
it put on record, so to speak, by you,. has made it doubly
precious. It did occur to me that you yourself might have
wanted it, had all this taken place a year ago and you had not

*moved to Maplethorpe. But I have a feeling you are getting
really dug in there, with all the improvements you are making.
Of course, if you DID have any thoughts about Ivers, you have
only to say. First refusal and preferential treatment. . . .*

I did not open the rest of my post for some little time, even
though I recognised Frederick Avery's handwriting on
one of the envelopes. I simply sat there at the kitchen
table, trying to digest the Tanners' news. Ivers without
them seemed unimaginable. I thought how lucky I had
been that they had been the owners when I was doing my
research. Although I had not seen a lot of them, they had
become real friends – and now they were off to the other
side of the world. There would be letters, of course, and
maybe the odd visit – for I knew Prue's parents lived in
Scotland – but that close link we had forged would be gone
or, at least, weakened.

As for Prue's tentative suggestion about my buying the
place, that, I knew, was out of the question. Ivers might
have had my interest, but Maplethorpe had my heart.
Besides, after all my experiences with the diaries, I did not
want to live under Great-Granny Alice's roof. Somehow,
with my two volumes launched, George gone and the
Tanners off to Australia, I felt as if a whole long chapter
of my life was closing.

But I certainly wanted to see Prue and her family again
before they left, even if I was not so keen to stay at Ivers.
It occurred to me that if only Maplethorpe was a bit more
habitable, they might come here. Then I thought how
madly inconvenient that would probably be for them, with
all the business of selling the house and packing up. I
could possibly persuade them to come for a day just to *see*
Maplethorpe, but it would seem most ungracious not to
accept Prue's offer of a last weekend at the house into
which I had initially more or less invited myself.

Oddly enough, Frederick Avery's letter also told me to
keep a look-out in *Country Life* in the coming weeks, when
he hoped his review of my second volume would appear.
I had had several letters from him lately, for he had been
sent – not without calculated foresight on Anthony's part

– one of the very earliest available copies back in the beginning of December, about which he had written to me enthusiastically. Subsequent reports from other sources all seemed to indicate that the book was doing well, even though the publication date had been a little on the late side for reviews before Christmas. Nevertheless, such encouragement had made me think quite seriously about writing the novel Anthony had suggested. A vague idea had been forming in my mind and I knew from past experience that I ought to get something down on paper, especially as Adam had gone to spend a week with Julian in the north and the alterations at Maplethorpe – which had been in abeyance over the Christmas period – had reached a point where there was little I could do personally, except supervise.

Yet, with that strange perversity which I had come to understand all too often prevents would-be writers of books actually sitting down to write them, I decided to sidestep the issue and answer Prue's letter instead. It was well into mid-morning before I managed to force myself, mentally and physically, to put some blank sheets of paper on to my clip-board and scrawl, with misgiving, Page 1, Chapter 1 at the top of the first one.

But somehow, after that, it didn't seem quite so bad. By four o'clock that afternoon, when I left off to post Prue's letter, I reckoned I must have clocked up two or three thousand words. True, it didn't look like much and getting them down at all had been punctuated by long pauses and a welcome break for bread and cheese and coffee. God knows where they all came from. As I walked up the lane to the pillar-box, I couldn't help thinking of Gregory Fawcett and his 'somewhere other' theory, although I couldn't quite go along with Frederick Avery's assertion that because Time was all one, the stories were always *there*, simply waiting for someone to stretch out and catch hold of them and write them down. That really did seem a bit far-fetched.

Yet, as the month went by and the novel began to take shape, when I was in bed at night I thought a lot about this creation business and the extraordinary characters who had arrived, unbidden, into my narrative: the recluse, who I felt bore some resemblance to Frederick, the rector's wanton daughter – now wherever did she come from? – his clever reserved son, the imperious lady of the manor who reminded me of my company commander in the ATS. She was *really* beginning to take hold, bossing me about and organising the story in a way I had not dreamed of.

There were, of course, many times when I would stop and think: whoever is going to want to read this? But then, although not my strong point, a certain logic would come to my rescue. I would say to myself: What would you be doing if you weren't writing? It's keeping you occupied, you aren't harming anyone, it's helping you not to miss George quite so much, you're not wasting any money or hitting the bottle or any of the things which sometimes affect people living alone. And if the worst comes to the worst and Anthony Webster turns the book down, it'll be disappointing but not the end of the world.

I went to spend the promised weekend with Prue at the end of February, a time of year when I had stayed at Ivers once before. I found the children had grown out of all recognition. Caroline was going through a shy stage, but confided in me that one day she would return to England, where she intended to 'write books like you, Mrs Vicky'. When I asked her what they were to be about, she became silent for a while before coming out with 'The lady who lived here before'. I did not press her further. It seemed to me that Prue's youngest daughter – alone of all the family – must have had some kind of rapport – I could think of no other word – with Great-Granny Alice.

On the Sunday afternoon, I felt this to be confirmed, when Caroline came and sat on my bed while I was packing my suitcase prior to leaving. During the weekend she seemed to have completely lost her shyness and had been following me around. Flattered, I asked her if she would write to me from Australia.

'Oh, *yes*,' came the immediate reply, 'and I'll draw you pictures, too.'

'That would be lovely,' I said. 'I'll look forward to that.

I shall want one of the house where you live so that I can picture you all in it.'

'All right,' she answered and then, to my surprise, added, 'What's artistic licence?'

I wondered where she had heard the phrase. Slowly, I began to explain that artists were allowed to put things into their pictures so that the final result was not just like a photograph, but how they themselves felt and thought about whatever they were drawing.

'Is that what the artist did on the front of your book?'

I stopped, all but ready to close my case. The child had all my attention now.

'How do you mean?' I asked.

'Well, she made the lady outside the window just like you.'

That same strange ill-at-ease feeling began creeping over me once again. I thought I had got through the weekend well. It had taken little Caroline Tanner to make me realise how vulnerable I still was.

27

While Adam was taking his A-Levels that summer, I invited Janet and her daughter for what was becoming their annual holiday – although I hardly liked to call it that, considering the work the former put in every time she came to Maplethorpe.

When they had come before, Vera, being unable to manage the stairs, had always slept in the sitting-room. Now, I was able to offer them the use of the separate extension which I had had made for Adam. I felt slightly guilty about this, looking at it from Adam's point of view, but he had never been a boy to mind about such things, always generous to a fault with his possessions, his time and his willingness to put others before himself. Often, I marvelled at how lucky I was in having such a son and longing for George to be there to witness the way he was developing.

I did not expect him to do brilliantly in his exams, but I was not worried about this because of his extraordinary dedication to pursuing the career he had chosen. What seemed infinitely more important was how well liked he appeared to be with both masters and boys and, indeed, the old and young in any community. Julian Wainwright was still his best friend, although now we had moved permanently to Maplethorpe, Adam and Robert Colbert saw a lot of each other in the holidays.

I found myself relying more and more on Diana's friendship and thinking that, although ten years older, she bore, in character, such a striking resemblance to Prue Tanner. I had taken Diana into my confidence about Janet and Vera and while they were staying with me she often called in. I think we were both very conscious that our respective sons had now passed their driving-tests and the sight of Vera in her wheel-chair – although her condition had not been caused by a car accident – somehow affected us deeply.

I had already sent Janet some of my manuscript for typing, but that June she immediately got down to the rest which was ready, sometimes talking to me about it after she had seen her daughter safely into bed for the night. Janet was the only person I would ever have let see my work at this stage and, had it not been for my reliance on her typing skill, intuitiveness and utter integrity, I would have preferred to keep the whole thing to myself. I was aware that other writers often submitted synopses, or even chapters, to their publishers or agents for help and guidance as they went along. It might have appeared arrogant of me not to want to do this, but I think it was really due to a sense of insecurity. If I received adverse criticism I doubted I should have had the courage to continue; even if it were constructive criticism, I also doubted I would have been willing to take it. And if there happened to be a favourable report, I believe I should have become suspicious. Before embarking on the writing game, I had never been a particularly secretive person, but now I felt that what I was doing was extremely personal. I was aware that my odd experiences – which I had never divulged to anyone other than Frederick Avery – when I was so involved with Great-Granny Alice, probably had a lot to do with this. But whatever the reason, I felt the novel I was now writing was mine and mine alone. When it was finished would be the time for it to stand or fall, according to the judgement of others.

One evening, when Janet and I were sitting out on the loggia I had created – where, in its more primitive state, I had often worked on the diaries – she said to me, 'Have you thought what you are going to call your new book?'

I hesitated. It was something which I kept turning over in my mind. Somehow, tonight, there seemed no reason why I should not at least try out my idea on Janet.

'I'm not sure, but I thought of *The Presentiment*.'

'I think that's good. I get the feeling all the time that something pretty momentous is going to happen. I wouldn't dream of asking you what. In any case, that would completely spoil the suspense, but I just can't wait to type the end.'

'Really? I'm glad, but I'm afraid you might have to wait quite a while, and you know I'm not absolutely certain what's going to happen myself. Sometimes I feel as if I'm looking forward to finding out, too.'

She laughed. 'But I bet it gives you a sense of power, doesn't it, shoving people around?'

'Some of the characters insist on shoving themselves but, yes, I see what you mean. The story can so easily be *diverted* this way or that. When I was a child I remember never wanting to choose which route we should take or even where we might go on some outing. I mean, one way might lead to . . .' I hesitated, remembering poor handicapped Vera, but it was too late. 'To some kind of disaster,' I went on. 'But if one took another,' I added quickly, 'something nice might happen.'

'When do you think you'll finish?'

'Hard to say. Having you here typing is certainly spurring me on, but when Adam comes home from school for good, bringing a friend for the holidays, I'll probably find myself slowed up considerably.'

'He's a dear boy, isn't he? You know, I can't help thinking of him as my nephew. I mean . . . well, if things had been different.'

We became silent. It was getting quite dark now, a blue black sky creeping down over the trees at the top of the garden. The scent of roses mingled with that of new-mown hay from one of the Colberts' nearby fields. I got up and went indoors, where I poured us each a small glass of brandy.

When I returned, I could tell that Janet was still thinking about Howard. We didn't say very much and I sat there picturing their last meeting, the dancing, the heightened emotion created, but overshadowed, by the coming parting. How ghastly it must have been for her: the pregnancy quite alone, my brother never knowing, his death at Alamein, her mother's rejection of both her and the baby. And now, this grown-up daughter, Vera, who, through some tragic accident, had reverted to babyhood again. How had Janet managed to stand up to it all, to remain such a splendid uncomplaining person? I couldn't have. It seemed to me that she had learnt something. I wasn't quite sure what it was, but I felt she was a great deal wiser, older

– though not in years – than I was and also possessed of infinite compassion. It would appear that she was one of those rare individuals who, through suffering herself, knew just how to give out to others.

Shortly after I saw her and her daughter off in the special ambulance car I had managed to arrange for them, Adam and Julian came back to Maplethorpe prepared to celebrate the end of their schooldays and final exams. They were two young men who seemed to complement each other: Julian the more erudite, hoping to get to Oxford to read History, Adam, the more artistic, creative, looking forward to going to Sandalheath Manor that autumn. Both of them were full of the immense hope and optimism of youth.

Yet, despite this, they were eager to fill in their holidays by doing whatever temporary work they could find. Owing to increasing mechanisation, Edward Colbert had no need of casual labour during harvest. His son, Robert, was already driving a second combine, but it so happened that Edward was having a new grain silo installed and the local agricultural engineers, anxious to get the job done by the end of August, were willing to take on Adam and Julian as long as they got themselves properly insured for a few weeks. Sometimes, if the three boys came to feed at Maplethorpe at the end of the day, I noted with interest that it was Robert who, while not having had such a broad or academic education as the other two, was infinitely the most mature. He would be able to step into his father's shoes splendidly when the time came.

'Although Edward's thinking of sending him off to work his way round the world after Christmas,' Diana told me one evening, when all the boys had gone into Weymouth to some disco. 'I must say, I shall hate it, but I suppose one has to let them go. And now Sue keeps on about being an air hostess. Motherhood's never without its worries, is it?' Then, thinking that she had perhaps been insensitive, she added, quickly, 'Oh, I'm *sorry*, Vicky. Forgive me. You're all alone and you've only got the one.'

'Yes, but don't forget I'm lucky in that Adam doesn't seem to want to do anything else but wood-carving and he'll be very close at Sandalheath.'

'Yes, I'm glad of that. I suppose it really was Herbie who started him off on that track, wasn't it? Odd to think that if you hadn't come to Pennyford in the holidays, Adam might have become interested in something completely different. Incidentally, poor old Herbie doesn't look at all well these days, does he? Since his wife died, he seems to have lost all his usual zest for living. Mrs Markby did what she could for him last winter, but I think she doubts he'll get through another. His chest has never been his strong point.'

'I know. I'm very sorry. Adam went to see him as soon as he came home, as he always does, and he was quite shocked at the way he seems to have aged since Easter. I'll drop in on him myself again tomorrow.'

I went to see him the following afternoon, taking with me a pot of honey and a copy of his favourite magazine which, surprisingly, was *The Illustrated London News*. I knew that he had been born in Clapham, where his father had been a cabinet maker who had died young from consumption. With scarcely any money and anxious to get her somewhat delicate son away from the metropolis, with all its pea-soup fogs, his mother had thrown herself on the mercy of her late husband's sister and come to live with her and her husband in Pennyford, where she earned a living as a seamstress. In due course, Widow Ems died and Herbie, a gangling lad of fifteen, was taken on by the previous owner of Warreners Farm, where it quickly became apparent that, as far as wood and carpentry were concerned, he had inherited the skills of his late father. Ten years later, with the promise of his own cottage, he had married the elder sister of Mrs Markby, who, since his wife died, now 'did' for him out of family loyalty and the goodness of her heart.

I found the old man much frailer than when I had last seen him only ten days previously. But he was dressed and shaved and greeted me with his usual grave courtesy. With his snow-white hair and finely chiselled features, I couldn't help thinking – as I had many times before – that, somewhere along the line, the Ems family must have had some kind of affiliation with the aristocracy and Bessie

Shergold and the Honourable Frank Dewhurst came once more to mind.

We sat chatting for half an hour or more. He told me, as he often did, what a fine son I had. He said he thought that Sandalheath Manor was a good establishment 'from all accounts', although he hoped they wouldn't start 'Mr Adam' – as he insisted on calling him – 'getting the wrong ideas about wood'. When I asked him exactly what he meant by this, he replied, 'You've got to *know* your wood. Wood's like an 'ooman. Sometimes it'll give and sometimes it won't. The hard kind can be made more pliable if you know how to work on it. 'Course, there's some woods best left alone. Personally, I don't care for elm. Shallow roots. You know the old saying? An elm tree always gets his man in the end. If it don't fall on 'im, it'll make his coffin.'

On the way back to Maplethorpe, I kept thinking about his last remark. Would they be putting Herbie into an elm wood coffin before long? And then, following on from that sombre reflection there came, against my bidding, the horribly hard and practical thought: might I be able to acquire his cottage for Janet and Vera?

28

Mrs. Markby's prediction regarding Herbie Ems proved all too true. That winter there happened to be a particularly virulent form of 'flu sweeping the country. Along with many another more robust pensioner, he was carried off to his Maker in the middle of January.

Herbie's funeral – to which Adam drove over from Sandalheath – was attended by what seemed to be the whole of Pennyford, as well as plenty of other local inhabitants from the surrounding district. I sat in the church, immensely saddened by the passing of someone who had come to mean so much to me and my son over the years, thankful that at least I had been able to put in a word about his coffin, which was made of deal.

That evening, before Adam returned to college, I thought I would talk to him about Herbie's cottage. It may have seemed like indecent haste to broach the subject then and there, but I knew I would have to act quickly on two counts. One was because it was obvious that there would be more than one person who, aware of the ever-decreasing need for farm staff, would probably be asking Edward about it. The other was because I had yet to find out whether Janet would accept my offer, even if I was able to make it.

Adam was enthusiastic about the idea, quickly making practical suggestions as to how Downside – as the cottage was called – could be adapted to suit the needs of Vera, even going as far as to say that he would be willing to undertake the alterations himself during the holidays.

'Why don't you go and call on Edward as soon as I've gone,' he said. 'I ought to be getting back now. I'll drop you off at Warreners on my way.'

So, half an hour later, I found myself sitting in the Colberts' drawing-room explaining the reason for my visit and saying I hoped I wasn't being too precipitate. As I expected, they were only too pleased at the thought of my purchasing the cottage which, since Herbie's retirement, they had let him continue to occupy at a peppercorn rent.

'But only,' I insisted, remembering Prue Tanner's remark about preferential treatment, 'if you let me have it at full market value. I'll do my best to find out Janet's reactions as soon as possible, so as not to mess you about.'

I drove to Southampton the next day. To my surprise and consternation, she broke down completely when I told her what I had come about.

Hitherto, Janet had always struck me as a person who kept her emotions under control, even though she sometimes found it difficult. I was puzzled by this reaction, especially as it was not exactly one of pleasure or gratitude but more like anguish. When she had had time to calm down a little, she began, bit by bit, to explain her predicament.

'I nearly confided in you last summer,' she said, 'but I didn't really have much to go on then. Just a hunch. It wasn't until Christmas that I knew for sure and it's been worrying me ever since. You see, I've had a proposal of marriage. There's this man, Bill Tranter, who once owned the laundry where I used to work. He's quite elderly now. His wife died a year ago and he's . . . well, lonely. He'd like to marry me and he's willing to take on Vera too. I like him and respect him, but I don't *love* him, of course. I've told him this and he says he quite understands. He's very kind and he's well-off and generous. I know he'd never let Vera or me want for anything. He's quite prepared to wait for me to make up my mind. In the meantime, he just keeps dropping in for a meal, because I can't go out. He always brings something with him, a bottle of wine, a steak, all sorts. I had him here for Christmas lunch. It was then he proposed.'

So *that* was the friend Janet had said she would be entertaining, when I had asked her what plans she had for that day.

'I don't know what to do, Vicky. I truly don't. If I did accept Bill's offer I feel it would let you off the hook, but it would be like marrying for a meal ticket, wouldn't it?'

Poor honest moral Janet. I tried to explain that I had never felt in the least *on* the hook. But I could understand her dilemma. Now, far from helping her, I seemed to have added to her problems. Bill Tranter could obviously make her more secure than I could. But it was a decision only she could make. I thought perhaps it was best not to stay too long and leave her to wrestle with this unexpected new development.

As she came to the door with me, she said, 'Even if I don't marry Bill, I've felt for a long time it isn't right to let you go on subsidising me as you do. I wish to God I was more independent.'

'Look,' I replied, 'Forget about that. I'm your sister-in-law and Vera is my niece in all but name. And, as you once remarked yourself, you look on Adam as your nephew. From our point of view, it would be lovely to have you at Pennyford. You've been the greatest help to me and your friendship means more than I can say. Naturally, there's a bit of urgency about the cottage, but the Colberts are very forbearing and no one wants to point a pistol to your head. Just give me a ring as soon as you can.'

I left her. A biting wind hit me as I walked to the car. Whatever Janet decided, I longed to see her away from the place in which she was living.

In the end, the decision, as perhaps happens in life more often than not, was taken from her. She phoned me three days later to say that Vera had succumbed to the same 'flu which had carried off Herbie. She was in hospital and on oxygen. Because of her physical immobility, her condition was grave.

Within thirty-six hours, Vera was dead.

I was unsure whether Janet would like me to be with her and relieved when my offer to do so was accepted gratefully. I realised that she was not nearly the calm, sensible, self-reliant person which she appeared to be to the rest of the world. I stayed with her for a week, during which Vera was buried and I managed to pack up and dispose of all the reminders of her presence in that small inconvenient house, including the girl's wheel-chair. At the end of that time, I suggested that Janet might like to return with me to Maplethorpe for a while. But this offer, she definitely declined.

She told me before I left that her daughter's death had made her see things more clearly.

'It wouldn't be honest if I didn't admit it's a great relief, Vicky. I realise that by accepting help from you or Bill Tranter I was thinking of it only because of Vera. I shan't marry him now and, kind and tempting as your generous offer seems which you've said you still stand by, I wouldn't be happy letting you buy Downside for me. I'm free at last and I can go back to work. I don't quite know what it'll be, but I'll find something. I desperately want to be independent. I'd still love to type anything you write but, please, from now on there must be no more hand-outs. Incidentally, how are you getting on with *The Presentiment*? I've been so taken up with my own troubles, I quite forgot to ask.'

'Slowly,' I replied. 'As I think I told you last summer, I'm not exactly what you might call a prolific writer. I have to let it come to me and sometimes it . . . well, doesn't.'

'But you must be longing to get back to Maplethorpe, just in case. I shouldn't have let you do all you have.'

'Rubbish, I don't see why not,' I answered, finding such gratitude always somewhat embarrassing.

On the way home, I realised that, Janet being Janet, she could not have possibly chosen any other course than she had and by becoming independent again she would find far greater happiness than being the recipient of any material security, which the poor woman had only ever sought because of her daughter. I could not see her marrying Bill Tranter now, nice as I had found him to be when we met at Vera's funeral. Neither could I really see Janet at Downside, even though she would doubtless have got herself some sort of job in or around Pennyford. No, I knew that, much as I should have enjoyed having her as a neighbour, I must let her go her own way and that, once she had become a little more firmly established, I would probably have to accede to her request and cease making 'hand-outs', as she called them.

I was surprised to see a light on at Maplethorpe as I turned down the lane and, as soon as I drew up outside, the front door opening and Markie standing in the hall

with what looked like a piece of paper in her hand. For
one ghastly moment, I thought her presence might have
something to do with Adam.

'It's all right,' she called, as I flung myself out of the car
and ran towards her, taking what I could now see was the
telegram she was holding out but which, thank God, was
a Greetings one.

'Came this afternoon,' she went on. 'Archie didn't quite
know what to do with it as you weren't here, so I said I'd
hand it to you, personal like, as soon as you got back.'

Even as she spoke, I was tearing at the envelope, all
decorated with flowers and cherubs: 'Sold paperback rights
of *Great-Granny Alice* STOP Writing STOP Felicitations.
STOP Ruby.'

I sat down suddenly on the small chair just inside the
door. I remembered the time when I had first received
Ruby Thetford's appreciative letter about the diaries. Then,
recovering a little, I became aware of Markie looking at
me, expectantly.

'It's from . . .' I nearly said 'my agent,' but it sounded
so pompous. 'It's just to tell me that something to do with
my great-grandmother will be printed in paperback,' I
ended up, rather lamely.

'Really? Fancy that. Now look, Mrs Vicky.' Markie's
thoughts turned at once to what she considered much
more important matters, 'I've made you a shepherd's pie,
so I'll just go and pop it in the Aga. And Mr Colbert says
to tell you he thinks we're in for some snow. If you hadn't
got back tonight he told me to turn the water off. I wish
to goodness that baby of the Gerrishes would hurry up.
I can mind how the ambulance got stuck coming over
Baldersby Hill when Mavis Gerrish had her last one two
years back.' Markie bustled into the kitchen, unconsciously
putting me firmly in my place. I was now working on my
third book, my first two were to be paperbacked, but in
Pennyford I was simply Mrs Norbury – or Mrs Vicky, as
many people called me – mother of Adam, owner of
Maplethorpe, reasonably well liked – or so I hoped – but
as for being an *author*, that was some curious kind of
sideline which kept me out of mischief in my spare time.

29

Due to the weather, I was incommunicado for over a week. The telephone wires were down and some days the post didn't get through. On those when it did, the sight of Archie Turnbull struggling down the lane was extremely welcome, particularly when he arrived with a letter from Ruby and another from Anthony.

Ruby's was, as I anticipated, full of delight and excitement. Anthony's proved even more so. The former quoted what I considered to be an astronomical figure for the paperback sale, together with a rough idea of the details and provisos to be incorporated in the contract I would be receiving and which I was sure I would not understand. Both letters ended on a slightly more ominous note: *How is the novel coming along*? Yet, even that, for the moment, seemed of no consequence. My attention was elsewhere.

Two days later, Archie brought me quite a batch of mail. I sat by the kitchen window, opening the most interest-looking envelopes first. Outside, it was Christmas-card land, the garden all white and glistening under a clear blue sky. Icicles hung from the loggia and I wondered whether the honeysuckle I had planted in one of the tubs would survive. I was immensely thankful for the central heating I had installed, as well as the fact that the oil man had filled up the tank just before I went to stay with Janet. I felt warm and snug as if I were in some kind of igloo, cut off from the rest of the world except for the lane leading down to it through which Edward, bless his heart, had sent a caterpillar tractor and lifting-apparatus to clear a path. If it were not for the fact that I could not help basking in the euphoria created by my unexpected news, it would have been an excellent time to get on with my novel. Being unavoidably incarcerated in one's own home, without interruptions, should have been ideal for the job. However, today, the only thing I intended to compose were answers to my various correspondents.

There was an airmail one from Australia which demanded immediate attention.

> *Dear Mrs Vicky,*
>
> *I am very sorry not to have written before to thank you for the lovely book you sent me for Christmas, but I think Mummy has told you that I broke my arm riding.*
>
> *I still don't like this house as much as Ivers. It is in a very noisy street, but Mummy and Daddy say we will be moving more into the country soon. Also that she will bring us to England next year for a holiday, when you are having your summertime. It is funny to think you will be reading this in your winter. I wonder if you have any snow???*
>
> *The other day when we were in a bookshop I saw GREAT-GRANNY ALICE on the shelf and the lady like you going by her window. I wonder what you will write next. I am going to call my first book IVERS and do the drawings all myself.*
>
> *I hope you are well.*
>
> > *Lots and lots of love,*
> > *Caroline*

There then followed a row of kisses and a somewhat horrendous picture of the writer coming off her pony. Thank God she was not more hurt. Would she, I wondered, really be an author when she grew up or would such an ambition fall by the wayside? I hoped not. She was obviously a child with great originality of thought.

The next letter I opened was from Janet. *I tried ringing you two nights ago*, she wrote,

> *but found your telephone must have gone o.o.o. due to the snow. Thank goodness you were able to use it the night you got back and tell me that wonderful news about GREAT-GRANNY ALICE. I am so terribly PLEASED, but then, I always knew you were on to a winner there.*
>
> *I do hope you're not too cut off, Vicky, but I have a feeling the Colberts wouldn't allow that to happen. Drop me a line when you can. I'm relieved to think you went home when you did, but I'll never be able to thank you enough for all the help*

*and support you gave me when you were here, nor indeed, for
ALL you have done for me for such a long time.*

*I've already started making enquiries about a job. There is a
new agency starting up which seems promising. It caters for
people wanting temporary help in crises. You know, part
nursing, child care, cooking etc. I think I'm fairly well qualified
and it would suit me because the work would be varied and not
permanent, so if one got somewhere and didn't like it one would
know it wasn't for ever. I quite like the idea of getting about a
bit and it would be easy to shut this house up for a few weeks
and let my neighbour have the key to look in now and then! I'll
keep you informed . . .*

All I could think was that whoever got hold of Janet in an
emergency such as she described would be lucky. But I
could see that, although she seemed to have spent her life
looking after others, it probably *was* a job which would
now suit her down to the ground. I liked the thought of
her getting around and out of that cramped confined
atmosphere in which she had been living for far too long.

The rest of my mail looked like bills or business letters
except for one rather grander envelope containing a stiff
card, which I found was an invitation to a reception in
London to mark the publication of Professor Avery's latest
historical work, *Generals Down The Ages*. A PTO had been
scrawled at the bottom and, on turning it over, I found he
had written: *Do come if you can and dine with me afterwards.
A copy of the book is on its way to you, although I doubt it's your
cup of tea. How is the novel?* I began to wish I had never told
anyone I was even attempting to write one.

I turned the card over once again and noted the date of
the reception. Three weeks away. The snow would surely
be gone and a trip to London might be rather nice. I could
stay at my club or even with Jill Patterson, see Anthony
and Ruby and do a little shopping.

There was a sudden tapping at the window and I looked
up, startled to find Adam outside grinning at me.

'What on *earth* . . . ,' I said, opening the back door.

'One of the tutors was coming this way in a Land Rover.
The snow isn't nearly so bad round Sandalheath. I said I

was worried about my mother and he volunteered to give me a lift. I've promised to meet him at the top of the lane at two o'clock. I dare say I could cadge a lunch off you.'

I smiled. I was so enormously pleased to see him – and touched. Adam really was a son in a million, turning out to be just as George had predicted. We spent a good morning. I was able to tell him about the paper-backing of *Great-Granny Alice* and of Janet's decision and he was able to tell me that a replica of an antique bureau on which he had been working was going to be shown at the Bath Academy of Art in the summer.

'You know, when I leave Sandalheath,' he said, 'I was wondering whether I couldn't make a real go of that sort of thing. Of course, I'd have to have a show-room somewhere, maybe start off by renting a window in some town, but doing the work here. It would need a lot of thinking out. But I'm told Americans love hand-carved miniatures. Go crazy about them. Apparently, there was a man near Salisbury they used to flock to see whenever they visited the cathedral. He must have been unique. I wish I'd known him. They seem to think at Sandalheath I might, well . . . try to do something of the same sort.'

He was so young, so enthusiastic, but I remembered that it was Emerson who said that nothing ever got done without enthusiasm. Knowing how long it had taken him to finish this model, which he had begun on arrival at Sandalheath, I thought, as George had done, that it was unlikely he would ever make much money. But what did that matter? He was my only son, he would inherit from me when I died and the thought of him actually living at Maplethorpe seemed too good to be true.

Yet I knew I would have to be careful. I could so easily let him become the man in my life and then, when he married, I would have to start all over again learning to live alone. I realised that some people might have said that the answer to that would have been to re-marry. But who? Anthony and I seemed to have gone past that stage. The only other unattached male I knew was Frederick Avery and the idea of marrying him seemed as ludicrous as improbable. I felt no desire to live with any man even if any man wanted – which I felt highly unlikely – to live with me. It was no doubt ethically preferable to marry for companionship rather than a 'meal ticket', as Janet had referred to it, but lately I had found all the companionship I wanted through the characters I had created in my novel. I had lived with them, more or less slept with them. Under such circumstances I should make a most unsatisfactory proposition for any man to take on. I certainly wouldn't want to break off in the middle of writing in order to cook a man a meal. I would be prepared to do so for Adam because that was different. He was my son and now Maplethorpe had been enlarged we could remain separated, 'doing our own thing', as the modern generation put it. I did not feel we should get on each other's nerves. It would just be nice to know he was about.

I wished him goodbye a little before two o'clock and watched his retreating figure going up the lane. He had grown into a tall good-looking young man with a most engaging manner and delightful sense of humour. I knew that Sue Colbert, now nearly eighteen, secretly adored him, although I was not sure how much he was aware of this.

When he got to the top of the lane, he turned and waved and kept motioning me to go back inside. I don't know why I should have felt suddenly uneasy when I was once more back in the warm, but I did. It seemed to be vaguely connected with Adam, yet in some inexplicable way with the novel I had temporarily laid aside. The sensation was only fleeting, but it disturbed me.

Doing my best to shrug it off, I sat down at my desk and started to write to Caroline.

30

We sat in the lounge of the Hyde Park Hotel, Frederick having booked a table there for dinner, because he knew that the reception being given for him would go on too long for us to be able to comply with the old-fashioned rigid domestic timetable of the Athenaeum.

I thought he seemed nervous, several times running his finger round the inside of his shirt collar, fidgeting with his coffee-spoon and asking me twice if I would like another cup. We talked about *The Generals*, which by now I had read although, as he had rightly surmised, it was not exactly my cup of tea. However, I hoped I appeared adequately interested and appreciative.

After a while he brought the conversation round to my novel. I became evasive. Since Christmas I had virtually done no work on it and, whereas I might have picked up the threads again once my initial excitement about the diaries going into paperback had worn off, the curious unease I had experienced after saying goodbye to Adam that day in the snow had acted as a kind of not altogether unwelcome brake on proceedings. I was aware, all the time, of the manuscript lying in the top drawer of my desk, that I must go on with it, yet I was strangely averse to doing so.

One of Frederick's good points, I had discovered, was that although, like most authors, he was basically concerned about his own work, he did have the courtesy and tact to enquire about other people's, for I did not imagine for one moment that I was the only person in whose books he was interested.

However, looking back over the evening when I was in bed, I realised that I might have been wrong about this. Perhaps he *was* only interested in my creations after all. Because, quite suddenly, while I was doing my best to avoid saying anything very much about my novel – which was worrying me more than I cared to admit to anyone – he said, 'Would you find marriage incompatible with writing?'

The question, so unlike any of his others and coming so unexpectedly, caught me completely unawares. Even then, somehow I did not connect it with him personally. I felt it to be more of an academic enquiry than anything else. On the other hand, if I had been quicker, brighter and more in tune with my companion, I would have realised that it was of the greatest significance.

'Yes,' I answered, 'I think I *would* find the two difficult to combine. In fact . . .' I paused, unsure how to frame my next sentence. Then, I said, 'Before my husband's death, I realised that I often became far too wrapped up in the diaries, that I wasn't being fair to him. George was very good about it. He used to tease me sometimes. I wish I had been more aware of my short-comings as a wife.'

'But if husband and wife were *both* writers,' Frederick persisted, 'it might be different. They would respect each other's needs for privacy, that during the day work would keep them apart, notwithstanding that they were living under the same roof.'

He was looking at me very intensely now and it was quite obvious what he was getting at, even if it had been a funny way of getting round to it.

I suppose I was awfully unkind because I simply remained silent. I couldn't or wouldn't help him.

'I'm afraid I'm very bad at this,' he went on, hurriedly. 'I've never made a proposal of marriage before. Don't know the ropes. But I have long admired you and your work, Vicky. It would be such a very great honour if you would consent to becoming my wife.'

A waiter came and took away the coffee tray and enquired if we wanted anything else. I shook my head. When others, such as Markie, had sometimes said, 'You could have knocked me down with a feather,' I had merely looked on it as a funny little figure of speech. Now, it came to me with all its full meaning. Here was I, Victoria Norbury, sitting in the Hyde Park Hotel, being asked to marry a learned professor whom I had only met a few times, who had never even given me so much as a chaste peck on the cheek, whose relatives, home, habits and past life were completely unknown to me, as mine must be to him.

I did my best. I explained that much as I appreciated and was, indeed, tremendously honoured by his very kind offer, I did not intend to marry again – ever. I was used now to a somewhat lonely existence, albeit happily mitigated by my writing to which I wished to devote all my energies, apart from those which I gave to my son, when required. I told Frederick that I greatly valued his friendship and hoped we could continue this and that he might even visit me at Maplethorpe one day, when we could keep up our discussions on our mutual interest: Time.

He took it very well. He said he had rather thought that would be my answer. He was naturally disappointed but, yes, he would like to come to Maplethorpe, possibly in the summer when he was lecturing at Bristol University.

It was all most decorous, civilised and, I felt, infinitely sad. He escorted me by taxi back to my club, helped me out and, taking my hand, raised it to his lips.

It was in a sombre mood that I met Anthony next day for lunch. Compared to Frederick, he appeared so much younger, ebullient and full of the joys of spring. He began by congratulating me all over again on *Great-Granny Alice* going into paperback, he made a – mercifully – fleeting reference to my novel but then, quite suddenly, he became serious.

When the waiter had brought our cocktails, he asked me exactly the same question as Frederick had asked not much more than twelve hours previously.

'Do you think you would find marriage incompatible with writing, Vicky?'

This time I fear I must have done something quite unforgivable. Even Anthony seemed disconcerted. I burst out laughing.

Then, hastily excusing myself, I said, 'Please forgive me. It's just that . . . well . . . I was asked that only last night.'

He was quick. 'You mean by Frederick Avery?'

'Yes.'

'And what was your answer?'

I looked at him sitting opposite: so nice, so understanding, so infinitely more suitable a suitor than Frederick. 'It was "Yes, I would", Anthony,' I replied, levelly.

'And does that hold good for today? You see, I'll soon be a completely free man. My wife wouldn't consent to a divorce before. But we've lived apart for five years now and with the new divorce laws coming into operation, it'll only be a question of formality.'

For one agonising moment, I wavered. I liked Anthony so much. We had a lot in common, thought on the same wave length. I did not envisage that I would have any difficult with Adam, nor in respect of Anthony's teenage daughter. I even felt George would have approved. And Anthony would understand my need to write, more, probably, than Frederick, for he would be always wanting to spur me on to greater efforts, something which was sorely needed at the moment. I imagined he would keep his flat in town but would come to Maplethorpe at weekends, where he would fit in perfectly with the local community.

Such thoughts went through my mind, swift, clear, sharp and with what seemed like total logic.

And then, all at once, something, God knows what, made me stretch out a hand across the table and say, 'I'm so terribly sorry, Anthony. Yes, it still holds good today. But . . . thank you so very much for asking me.'

Looking back, I often wonder just why I did not accept Anthony's proposal there and then. Many was the time during the next few months, while I was struggling to finish *The Presentiment*, when I had a strong desire to lift the telephone receiver and ask if the offer was still open. But then I felt it would be cheating. I did not love Anthony *enough*. Janet's reference to a 'meal ticket' seemed to come into it somewhere. Not that I needed that. I was more than self-sufficient, but it would have been nice to have a shoulder to lean on as I grew older. But then I began to wonder whether it wasn't the very fact of advancing years that was actually holding me back. He and I had both travelled somewhat further along the road since the time when we had so nearly taken what Great-Granny Alice would have called 'the wrong turning'. I was by no means

sure how I would respond to all that side of life today.
Once one has reached a certain age, chosen, as it were, a
celibate path and has kept to it for some little way, any
other – or so it seemed to me – was not only inappropriate,
but vaguely ridiculous.

31

I sent off *The Presentiment* to Ruby in the middle of July. It had been a struggle to get it finished and I felt as if I had written the concluding chapters with my eyes averted from the page. Unlike the earlier part of the book, I did little or no revising, leaving it to Janet – who had come to type the end – also to make any corrections she thought necessary.

When the day came to put it in the post, she said, to me, 'It's awfully good, Vicky. Very powerful. I simply have to ask you, wherever did you get it all from?'

I replied, somewhat flippantly as I see it now, 'You'll have to ask Gregory Fawcett.'

'Who on earth's he?'

'Oh, someone I once met at a party. He says all creative work comes from "somewhere other". Sometimes I wish I'd never started on this writing racket. You're not mistress of your own fate any more. You get pushed around too much.'

She stared at me, rather oddly, I thought. 'I don't see that at all. I mean, you had all sorts of alternatives for the final . . . tragedy. Oh, granted, there *had* to be a death. But you had plenty of other ways for bringing it about.'

I searched in the kitchen drawer for some string. 'That's what I mean,' I replied, shortly, 'I wasn't given an alternative. Where are the scissors?'

The conversation came to an end.

I heard from Ruby within the week, from Anthony after the following weekend, during which he had apparently sat up into the small hours reading the manuscript from cover to cover. Both were full of enthusiasm for it.

I had no idea, Anthony wrote, *that you were engaged upon a psychological thriller. What a very dark horse you are, Vicky.*

It had not occurred to me that that was what *The Presentiment* was, but I realised such a description was probably a very fair one. Now that it was off my hands and to see print, I felt an enormous sense of relief. I chided myself for all my fears and doubts about completing it, particularly for allowing my uncontrollable imagination to get the better of me in connection with the story's ending. With what seemed like a very light heart, I turned my attention once more to Maplethorpe – this time to the garden.

There was a small stream which meandered by the lane leading down from the village and it occurred to me that this could be diverted to trickle in front of the rockery I intended making at the side of the house. It would simply necessitate the building of a small dam and this I proposed to do, with Adam's help, and a little cement that I believed I could get hold of from the road men.

'The County Council will be after you, Vicky.' Edward called out one morning, as he stopped his Land Rover on his way to see whether a certain field of wheat was fit for harvesting.

I smiled, put down the large flint I was carrying and went across to chat with him. I told him how much I was looking forward to having Adam home for the holidays and Edward, for his part, volunteered the fact that Robert, now settled at Warreners after his world trip, had the makings of a far better farmer than his father.

'He's so full of ideas, Vicky. I feel a back-number. Reckon I shall retire in a year or so and hand over the reins. Diana and I have our sights on Shacklebury End. It's the sort of sized house that would suit us down to the ground in our old age.'

I thought of Shacklebury, a small eighteenth-century manor situated, rather like Maplethorpe, in a little dell. I thought of Robert in charge at Warreners, Robert with a wife, with children. And Sue? Would she and Adam marry?

Then I checked myself. I mustn't let my mind run on like this. Our respective young were still so very young. They had so far to go. One must simply be thankful for them as they were now: their youth, charm, love of life and generosity of spirit. For they all had that – at least, all the ones I knew. They had time for their elders, if by no means betters.

I wished Edward goodbye and went back to my rockery and stream making operations.

That winter an idea for a short story came to me which

I sent to Ruby and which, to my surprise, was accepted by a women's magazine. It was simple enough and the undemanding genre suited my mood. I found myself undertaking various 'shorts' – as I called them – including one or two book reviews, although I was somewhat diffident about my qualifications or ability to judge other people's work. However, the remuneration was good and I was relieved of the burden of carrying out any long-term work, despite several veiled hints which came my way from Anthony.

He and his daughter, Avril, were coming to spend Christmas with Adam and me, and so was Julian Wainwright and Janet. With the four Colberts just up the lane I was looking forward to the event, carefully making dishes suitable for putting into the deep freeze so that I could spend the maximum amount of time with my guests.

It was a happy four days. I have many photographs of the occasion, but the scene engraved on my own private television screen is one of us all sitting round the dining-room table on Christmas night. I thought of it as a kind of 'still' – out of context. Even though only a little while ago I had been conjuring up visions of what the younger generation might be doing in a few years' time, now I wished we could all remain just as we were, rather as I recalled once having wanted to halt life when Adam was at the shorts-and-tricycle stage. I thought of Frederick's 'timeless moment' and felt that this, if ever there was one, was it. Everyone looked so happy. Or was that an illusion, brought about by the festive atmosphere, the wine, the goodwill?

After the holiday was over and my guests had all gone, I kept turning this over in my mind. Was Anthony still hoping to marry me? Sue was still surely eating her heart out for Adam who, I could not help noticing, was somewhat smitten by Avril who, in turn, seemed drawn to Robert. I had a sudden fierce desire to protect them all, to save them from whatever was in store. The unknown future rose up before me, dark and somehow sinister. What *was* it in me that made me so afraid, which seemed to invite disaster, that insisted on muddling up fact and

fiction? Where *was* it I had read that some authors aver
that, having invented certain incidents, they believe life
then says to them, 'Oh, that is how he/she likes it, is it?
Well, so be it.' Was *I* like that? Did I have a propensity for
bringing about things just because I saw them so intensely
in my mind's eye? No, of course not. It was a ridiculous,
fantastic supposition, one which I would never dare mention to a living soul. It was enough to brand me a mad
woman.

It occurred to me that perhaps I ought to go away, that I
had become altogether too introspective, too housebound,
too workbound. People went on cruises at this time of the
year, didn't they, not just the whoopee knees-up-Mother-
Brown kind, but rather unusual ones which took one up
the Nile, for instance. I even got as far as sending for a
few brochures but then, flicking through them one evening
by the fireside after Adam had returned to Sandalheath, I
thought I couldn't bear to leave Maplethorpe for a week,
let alone three, which seemed to be the minimum time I
saw advertised. Besides, I wasn't exactly a rubbernecker.
I was bad about being shown things. I suppose it was
arrogance, but I felt unhappy when engaged upon something which I felt to be entirely unproductive – unless, of
course, I could use the experience in a book. The idea of
being regimented each morning into looking at Egyptian
mummies appalled me, for I certainly couldn't imagine
ever wanting to write about them. Such pastimes – I always
thought the word singularly expressive – were not for me.

Although the trouble with you, I said to myself next day
as the idea for another short story started forming in my
mind, you don't really know what you *do* want.

32

It was Sue who told me all about it, but not until a long time afterwards – a year, in fact. I simply rang her up one evening and asked if she would come and see me because I wanted to talk to her about something. She knew immediately what it was. She'd always been quick. She said, 'Are you sure, Vicky?' – I had at long last got her to drop the 'Aunt' – and I replied, 'Quite sure, my dear.'

I can see her now as she sat on the loggia. She was wearing a full-skirted yellow cotton dress which she had designed and made herself. Such a pretty young woman she'd grown into. With her fair hair and bronzed skin, she seemed a kind of golden girl. It suddenly hit me that I simply hadn't been aware of the final growing-up of Sue, but then I hadn't been aware of a lot of things after that night when time really did stand still for me.

Almost up until it happened – the summer after my little Christmas house-party – I thought I'd been doing quite nicely. My short stories were selling well and because they were light, with happy endings – Ruby told me that women's magazine editors always insisted on giving their readers *hope* – they did not worry me or impinge on my own life in anything like the same way as my books had done.

I recall it was a particularly beautiful spring. I bought a little West Highland terrier whom Adam christened Rosie. The new cherry trees I had planted on either side of the front door were a riot of pink and white rosettes. The rockery, with its artificial cascade of water, looked as if it might have been there for ever and the daffodil bulbs I had planted earlier in the winter had more than come up to their name: Golden Promise. I had been extravagant with bulbs, not only in the garden itself but in the banks on either side of the lane.

'You've put us all to shame, Vicky,' Diana said, on coming down to visit me one day through a veritable aisle of yellow. 'We shall all have to start planting bulbs outside our own territory and turn Pennyford into a daffodil village like the one I was once taken to see in Hertfordshire. I hope you've got photographs of all this.'

'A few.' Somehow I didn't like to tell her that I had agreed to a reporter and a photographer, from one of the women's magazines for which I wrote, coming to Pennyford that week to do a feature on Maplethorpe. My writing activities and concentration on my own home somehow embarrassed me in the face of Diana and so many people around who seemed to do such much more worthwhile jobs.

We fell to talking, as usual, about our respective young and the dance the Wainwrights were giving that summer for Julian's twenty-first birthday. His father had recently returned to England for good and he and his wife had bought quite a large establishment some miles south of Oxford. This was where the dance was to be held and the house was to be thrown open for any of Julian's special friends who wanted accommodation for the night.

'Sue is just so thrilled about it,' Diana said. 'Thank God she turned against that air-hostess idea. She seems to be enjoying her fashion course at the local polytechnic. She's already started making her own dress for the Wainwright do. A most glamorous-looking creation it looks, judging by the sketches she's shown me.'

'I'm so glad.' I think we both knew that the real reason for Sue's change of heart over her career was that she wanted to stick around the district so as to be near Adam.

The first kind of set-back I had was about a month before the dance when Anthony sent me a rough for the jacket of *The Presentiment. We got Celia Merton to do it,* he wrote, *seeing that she had done so well with* Great-Granny Alice.

I remember my heart gave a nasty kind of lurch when I at last extracted it from the stiff envelope. There was no doubt it was good. Brilliant, in fact. I couldn't fault it in any way and to write back and say it gave me the shivers would be both crazy and discourteous. It was a 'seller'. There was no doubt about it. The fact that the young man Celia had drawn looked to me so very like Adam was neither here nor there. She had never even *seen* my son. I was imagining things. Once again, I told Anthony that it was fine and I would write and congratulate the artist on it as before although, this time, I did not offer to buy the original.

Spring had now given way to summer. The hum of a combine harvester seemed never far away. Tractors and empty trailers clattered down the lane from Warreners, returning more slowly, weighted down with corn. The Wainwright dance was to be on July 24th, a Friday. Adam was driving Sue up to Oxford that morning. Robert, busy with harvest, was driving up separately that evening. I understood that Avril had been invited, as well as a few other of their contemporaries whom I had got to know. On the Thursday, I met Sue in the village and there was a radiance about her that I have only ever seen once before, when a girl I shared a billet with in the ATS told me she had just become engaged to an Air Force pilot with whom I knew she was very much in love. I was sure now that Adam must have been aware of how Sue felt about him – he would have to have been blind not to – but I was worried. I knew that my son would never be unkind or thoughtless, but I also knew that Sue was desperately vulnerable. She could so easily get hurt.

They left quite early the following morning, with the intention of looking round Oxford and having lunch there. I was not expecting them back until the following night.

Although I was in the middle of a short story, I felt unable to write that day and I spent it gardening furiously, knowing that physical activity was always the best way of coping with the kind of mood I was in. I went to bed exhausted, but the sleep I had been hoping for did not come. I pictured the scene in Oxfordshire, saw Sue in her lovely creation – I had been privileged to a full dress rehearsal – saw her dancing with Adam, Avril with Robert. Or would it be vice versa. No, I couldn't allow brother and sister to dance together. Sue was, perhaps, dancing with Julian and, I hoped, plenty of other admirers. She certainly ought to attract them if she was looking anything like the vision which had pirouetted in front of me the previous week. Then, as often before, I told myself to stop trying to push people around. These young people had their own identity, their own lives to work out. They were not characters in a book or a story. They were flesh and blood. Real. They could take charge of themselves. Besides, even my own fictional beings never seemed to go exactly where I wanted them to.

I suppose I must have eventually dozed off, for the hands on my luminous clock showed four thirty when I awoke with a start. To this day, I don't know why. I was not aware of any sound save that of the faint rather comforting trickle of water cascading down the rockery. I got up, went across to the window and drew back the curtains. A brilliant moon bathed the whole of the garden in a clear white light, so clear that I could see individual flowers standing out as if sculptured by some ghostly hand. The scene was unreal and I was grateful for the heady scent of the sweet-smelling stocks I had planted to remind me that this was Maplethorpe, my home, which, in a few hours, would come to life in the most ordinary kind of way, with Archie bringing the letters and Markie arriving to do her Saturday clean-through.

I glanced across at Adam's Annexe – as we now called it – which, because of the high bank behind it, lay mostly in shadow. To my surprise, I saw there was a light coming from the window of the platform where he slept at the far end. I supposed that he had left it on, for he had been in a hurry to get away that morning. Yet it was unlike him. He was a methodical boy.

Slipping on a dressing-gown, I padded down to the kitchen where Rosie stirred, looked at me with one eye and curled up to sleep again. I had long since given up any hope of her making a house-dog. Then I took the keys off the hook on the dresser, let myself out and walked along the covered way to the Annexe where I opened the front door. The place was in complete darkness, save for a patch of moonlight now thrown on to the floor in front of me. I snapped on the electric switches one by one. They all lit up, except the one over Adam's bed where the bulb, presumably, had gone.

But had it done that during the brief time it had taken me to investigate? For that was the one I had definitely noticed shining when I had stood by my window. Or had I, in some way, been mistaken? Had the moonlight given the impression it was on? No, that was impossible. The moonlight was white and in any case not shining on that part of the Annexe where I had seen the square of *orange* light. I went back indoors and up to my window again. Everything was just as it had been a few minutes ago, except there was no light where I could have sworn I had seen one before.

I got back into bed, troubled. I did not sleep again. The telephone call came through at six-thirty and in some strange way I was ready for it.

Diana and Edward drove me up to the John Radcliffe Hospital at Oxford.

33

I never really gathered much about what happened at the time, only that after the dance Sue and Adam and Avril and Robert decided to go for a drive. Julian remained at home seeing off the last of his guests.

'It had been a good party, Mrs Norbury,' his father said. 'They weren't tired. Nor were they any the worse for drink. Nothing like that. They just didn't want the night to end. You know what the young are.'

'Yes.'

I sat with him in an ante-room at the Radcliffe, together with Edward and Diana and Anthony, who had driven straight down from London. I had been told that Sue and Avril and Robert were suffering from shock but Adam, my son, was dead.

'I am so very sorry, Mrs Norbury. So desperately sorry.' Julian's father covered his face with his hands. 'If only we'd never given the dance.'

'It wasn't your fault.' I found I was holding myself in, speaking peremptorily, almost conventionally. 'Where exactly did the accident happen?'

'At a small village about twenty miles from our home. Compton Ivers. I can't imagine what took them there.'

It was then I passed out.

I recall nothing about getting back to Maplethorpe. I was told afterwards that I spent several days as a patient at the Radcliffe, but I don't recall that either, simply that at some point I seemed to be in my own bedroom with Rosie curled up on my bed. There were faces bending over me: Diana and Edward, Sue and Robert, Julian, Anthony and Avril, Markie. I believe that Caroline and Prue Tanner – on holiday from Australia – turned up one day, too. And then there was Janet. She was there most. In fact, she seemed to be always there. Janet saying, 'Try to drink a little of this, Vicky.' 'What about a bath now?'

The local doctor came, I think, every day and once he brought an older man with him. Then an ambulance arrived and Janet told me I was going to a clinic in Bristol. 'Not for long, Vicky. Just until you're better.'

I must have been a sad disappointment to the doctors. I heard them discussing electric shock therapy over my body as if I weren't there. Perhaps I wasn't. I certainly didn't *feel* there. Or anywhere, for that matter. Janet told me later on that they decided against electric shocks. My memory was already too impaired. So I was brought home again.

Sometimes, as I passed my bedroom window I noticed leaves piling up on the grass below. I supposed in a vague kind of way it must be autumn or winter. It didn't matter which. It was all the same to me.

One weekend Anthony came alone and spent a lot of time just sitting in my bedroom not saying anything very much. I still wasn't really registering other people's reactions, but it struck me that perhaps he had something on his mind. On the Sunday, just before he left, he said, 'I've got the book, Vicky.'

'What book?'

'Your book. It's out now.'

I frowned. 'Oh, that,' I answered.

'Don't you want to see it?'

'No thanks.'

'The reviews are marvellous. Better than for *Great-Granny Alice*.'

'Are they? I wish I'd never written it.'

I suppose I hurt him, but I seemed unable to care.

He went away and later that evening Janet came and sat on my bed. She said, 'Vicky, dear, I do so want to help. I realise it was much easier for me when . . . Vera was struck down by that virus because I had to go on. I had to look after her. There was no one else to do it. But I often say to myself now: Thank God, Adam wasn't turned into a paraplegic. So much worse for a young man. I daresay I'm putting this awfully badly . . . but he'd have hated to see you like this. And dear Sue's so miserable about it. She loved him, too, didn't she.'

I stared at her. I had been so wrapped up in my own grief that I had forgotten what others had suffered.

'How long have I been like this?' I asked.

'Four months.'

Suddenly, I said, 'What on earth have you done for money all this time? The house . . . there must have been bills.'

She smiled. 'The Colberts and Anthony and your solicitor have taken care of a lot of things.'

'But you. You've given up all your other work.'

'Yes, of course. But you come first.'

I asked her to fetch my cheque book and wrote her a cheque which she protested was far too large, but which I eventually got her to accept. I think she did so in the end because she was so pleased that I had, as she put it afterwards, started to 'come to'.

I don't quite know when it was that Janet moved permanently into the Annexe. It just seemed to happen.

'Although if ever there comes a time when . . . you don't need me, Vicky, I'll . . .'

I cut her short. 'There won't be a time.'

'You never know. I've often wondered whether you might marry again.'

'Marry?' I looked at her incredulously.

She coloured. 'Anthony's so fond of you, you know.'

'But whatever sort of a wife d'you think I'd make?'

'A very good one, once you've recovered.'

'It's taking long enough,' I said.

And it was. Although I was able to undertake a few mundane tasks I seemed to be living in limbo, treading water, waiting for I knew not what. If it hadn't been for Janet and the Colberts and Anthony's visits, I think I might have given up altogether. A year went by. Warreners was in for another harvest. It was then that I asked Sue if she would come and see me. She had finished her fashion course and was due to go to London to share a flat with Avril in the autumn and work at a Design Centre.

I asked her if she would tell me all that she remembered about the accident, that is, if it wasn't too painful for her.

'No,' she said. 'It would be a relief. You don't know how much I've longed to. You see, I've felt so horribly guilty about it.'

'You? Guilty? How could you possibly be. Adam was driving, wasn't he?'

'Yes, but it was my idea to go . . . where we did. When we first got into the car we hadn't any idea where we wanted to head for. We just wanted to drive. It was the most glorious night. The moonlight made everything unbelievably beautiful. Adam had the hood of his car down. I remember we sang. All the songs they'd been playing at the dance. Beatles hits and a whole lot more. Suddenly I said, "How near are we to that place your mother wrote about in *Great-Granny Alice*?" And Adam replied, "Not far. Want to go there?" And we all chorused "Yes".'

'I don't think Adam knew much about Compton Ivers,' she went on. 'He said he'd only driven by it once, but he found the way quite easily. I remember we turned off up a lane past a stile and then he pointed out your great-grandmother's house standing there as clear as day with two huge trees on either side of it. I don't think I cared for it much. I don't know why. I suddenly felt rather frightened. We went on past the church, where he told us his ancestors were buried and then Adam said that if we just carried on we'd come to the main road again. He wasn't going at all fast. We rounded a corner and then, heaven knows why, he suddenly swerved. I heard him say, "Oh, my God." We hit a tree and that was . . . it. Rob managed to stagger to a nearby cottage and raised the alarm. I went with Adam in the ambulance. He was conscious for a little while, but only for a little.'

'Did he say anything else?'

'Only . . .' She hesitated. 'I'm not really sure about this. I don't suppose I ever will be. His voice was very faint, but I think he said he was trying to avoid a riderless horse.'

'Thank you, my dear,' I said. We sat very still then. Still and silent. I did not tell her how I, too, felt responsible for Adam's death. I did not think it would do any good and she might have thought it too far-fetched, simply a manifestation of my illness. I only said, 'You won't ever blame yourself again, will you, Sue? I believe . . . well, fate takes a hand in so much of life . . . and death.'

She got up to go. As she bent down to kiss me, I saw there were tears in her eyes.

I began gardening in earnest that late summer and autumn. It had been sadly neglected, although Janet had done her best. I worked long hours. The bank at the back of the house had become horribly overgrown and I spent many days hacking away at bramble and hawthorn. Then I turned my attention to the vegetable patch, digging where once upon a time I would have employed a little casual labour. Once or twice, Janet said, 'You won't overdo it, will you, Vicky?' I shook my head. The smell of earth had a pleasant tranquillising effect. I felt perhaps I was reverting to type. After all, I was the daughter of a market gardener who had had no literary aspirations whatsoever.

In the middle of October Anthony arrived for what was turning into a regular fortnightly visit. He said, 'I'm taking you for a weekend to an inn I know near Middlemarsh overlooking the Blackmore Vale.' I tried to protest. I hadn't been outside Pennyford for so long that the idea scared me. But he was adamant. 'It's all booked. It's a lovely spot, Vicky. We'll be able to do a bit of walking. I know you like to keep active these days.'

So we went. The place more than came up to expectations and the weather was glorious. We trudged miles, looking at the green and golden panorama spread out below us. It reminded me of the time Adam and I had picnicked near his school after George's death and my son had asked me if I believed in an after-life. I was glad I had answered, without hesitation, 'Yes'. Here, once again, eternity seemed to surround me. I felt suddenly and strangely comforted, as if decision-making had been taken from me. Was there something, after all, in what Frederick Avery had written about it being of no account if a man dies in youth? Selfishly, I realised I had only been thinking of Adam's death from my own point of view: the person who was left.

That night, sitting by the huge open fire back at the inn, Anthony said, quietly, 'You're never going to write another novel, are you, Vicky.' His words were more of a statement than a question.

'No,' I replied. 'But how on earth did you know?'

'Just a hunch.'

It struck me that he knew more about me than I had bargained for. Gradually, bit by bit, I began to tell him about my experiences connected with *Great-Granny Alice*, how I hadn't wanted to finish *The Presentiment*, how I often felt caught up in something beyond my control, but that I could usually summon up perfectly rational explanations for my fears if I put my mind to it.

'Why have you never confided in me before?' he asked.

'Because . . . well, I remembered what you once said about Lyonesse. I felt you'd think I was just imagining everything. Maybe I was. I don't know. A powerful imagination is the very devil. So hard to check.'

'Yes, but it's what makes you such a good writer. And, you know, when you hear of something like this from someone you know, as I know you, it puts a completely different light on it all. I feel that during intense creative activity or, if you prefer it, when you were under the influence of some powerful external force, you were subject to extraordinary experiences, time-dislocation, ESP, pre-cognition, past-into-present, call it what you will. I don't pretend to understand it, Vicky, any more than you probably do, but I accept that was what happened. Then, when that force was spent you returned to normal. I suspected that you weren't altogether happy writing, especially fiction, and now I am aware of the reason why you never want to do so again.'

For a while, we remained silent. Then, he continued, 'But as you're going to give up novel-writing you wouldn't have any problem over that other question I once put to you, would you? I mean, there would be no conflict regarding marriage.'

34

Anthony and I were married early the following year. There was, I came to realise, an inevitability about it, although right up until we went to the local register office, it seemed difficult to believe what was happening. Afterwards, I doubted that the marriage would ever have taken place but for the fact that he simply wouldn't take no for an answer.

There were still times when the loss of Adam engulfed me, black days when I did not want to talk to anyone and would shut myself away, albeit now not so much in my bedroom but in the seclusion of the enclosed vegetable patch, digging, planting or weeding furiously. In the end, I think it was because I felt I was being so ungrateful, not only to Anthony but also to Janet – who was very much on his side over the idea of marriage – which tipped the scales.

Both of us were in complete agreement that she must remain in the Annexe, however much she initially protested. For one thing, Anthony, though nearing retirement age, wished to continue working as long as possible and this meant he would be away during the week. 'I like to think you'll have company, Vicky, when I'm not there. It's important to me.'

The only concession he made to advancing years was that, urged by me, he agreed to travel to and from London by train rather than drive himself by car. 'I dare say you're right,' he admitted. 'It'll be less of a strain and I'll be able to get a hell of a lot more reading done that way.'

The other reason we wanted Janet to remain at Maplethorpe – apart from our genuine affection for her – was that Anthony had an idea of combining business with pleasure in the not-too-distant future and hoped to go to Australia, where I had no doubt that I would also be able to visit the Tanners. Janet, as custodian of Maplethorpe, would be invaluable. In fact, it was virtually impossible to visualise the place without her and the thought of the garden otherwise running riot during our prolonged absence appalled me.

Gardening had now become my great solace. I had managed to buy from Edward another quarter of an acre of more or less scrub land at the bottom of the existing boundary and this I was turning into a shubbery, complete with a winding walk and a stout oak seat at either end. It dawned on me that whereas at one time visitors and journalists had wanted to come to Maplethorpe primarily to see me, now they came to see the garden. I was a back-number and this suited me very well.

Gradually, its fame spread further afield. I was asked to give advice on the planning of other gardens, sometimes several counties away, while the magazines which had once published my fiction, now asked for practical articles on such matters as *Creating a Rockery*, *How To Tackle A Wilderness*, *Knowing Your Soil* and so forth.

'Just think,' Anthony said one Friday evening, after he had got down from London and we were sitting in the shrubbery together, 'I'm married to a *professional* gardener.' He appeared to take great pride in this.

'Well, at least it seems a much more worthwhile and rewarding occupation than weaving stories,' I replied. 'And awfully therapeutic. Ruby rang up earlier this week and asked for an article on just this angle. She wants me to put gardening forward as so much preferable to tranquillisers.'

He smiled. Never once did he mention my defection from the kind of career he had once envisaged for me. For this, I silently blessed him.

We had kept our wedding almost secret apart from our closest friends, but I thought perhaps it would be only courteous to write Frederick a letter, seeing that I had once assured him that I would be unable to combine writing novels with matrimony. I was glad to be able to tell him, in all sincerity, that I had given the former up. He wrote me a charming letter in reply, if perhaps slightly pedantic, wishing me well and expressing his gratitude for my re-newed invitation to come to Maplethorpe, which he said he would certainly like to do when next he was lecturing in the west country. But, once again, he never came.

Occasionally I saw references to him in the press and

once I noted that A. R. Thornton had written an usually interesting book entitled *The Myth Of Time*. But I did not buy a copy or get one out of the library. I desperately wanted to lead as normal a life as possible. If I had strayed, inadvertently, into the kind of realm about which Frederick wrote, that was all in the past; and if ever I allowed myself to think about the strange experiences that had then come my way – which I seldom did – I concentrated on every conceivable rational explanation for them.

Anthony and I went to Australia the following autumn, just in time for that country's spring, which was beautiful. The Tanners, now firmly established in a large, almost English-style, country estate just outside Melbourne, welcomed us with open arms. In fact, I stayed most of the time with them, while Anthony went about his business both in Melbourne and in Sydney. Their two eldest children were both living in the former city, pursuing their respective careers, one an aspiring actress, the other training to be a doctor. Caroline, still at home but in her last year at school, was enchanting: a mixture of great intelligence and that childlike innocence that I remembered so well. She was still determined to write and I did nothing to dissuade her. When she asked me why I had given up, I murmured something about illness, however much I disliked using it as an excuse.

We returned to England before the weather became unbearably hot, travelling part of the way by sea. Although, in many ways, the voyage was relaxing, I found myself willing the boat to make more speed, for I could hardly wait to get back to Maplethorpe.

On our return, we had many visitors, but one in particular meant much to us. Sue came to spend a weekend at Warreners and asked if she could invite herself for dinner that Saturday night. There was about her now a maturity, a wisdom which I had rarely seen in one so young. Hers was a sad face, but it occasionally lit up as if she were suppressing some inner happiness which had come to her at last.

We did not have long to wait to hear about it.

'I wanted you to be the first to know, apart from the

parents,' she said. 'We postponed any announcement until you got back. You see, Julian and I are engaged.'

I got up and kissed her. Julian had been Adam's best friend. I could think of no better news than that he and Sue were to marry.

'Although I'm afraid it may mean a spell of living in America,' she continued. 'Julian's been offered a post at Harvard next year. Still, the parents have an idea of doing a little travelling later on, especially as . . .' She stopped suddenly and clapped her hand to her mouth. 'Forgive me,' she said. 'I'm jumping the gun.'

I think we all guessed what she had almost let slip, but it wasn't for another month or so before it was confirmed. Edward and Diana would be moving into Shacklebury End in the autumn when Robert would be marrying Avril. For Anthony this was a wonderful bonus, for it meant he would have his only daughter living just up the road.

I never thought of visiting Ivers again and I don't suppose I ever would have, but for the fact that, some years later, I happened to be passing so close and suddenly had a desire to do so. There was, I think, possibly an element of wanting to test myself by going back. I had been approached by a young couple near Abingdon who, having acquired a new house, were at a loss to know what do do with the two acres of field that went with it. I did not make many such sorties these days, but they had visited Maplethorpe and were so anxious for my advice that I agreed to try to help them. I then arranged with Fred, from the local garage, to drive me, as he had done for some time now whenever I travelled any long distances.

I spent a good two hours going over their property and discussing various alternatives with them, after which they gave me an excellent lunch. Had it not been for the fact that I knew Julian's parents were away, I should almost certainly have then called in on them. As it was, I had the rest of a glorious September day in which to return, leisurely, to Pennyford. Fred was well aware of my dislike of speed.

Almost as soon as I had asked him to turn off to Compton

Ivers, I regretted it. Moreover, I felt that Anthony and Janet would disapprove. But then I took hold of myself. Surely I was a person in my own right now, wasn't I? I was leading my own life or, rather, a new kind of life with Anthony. I had freed myself from that other indeterminate hypothetical one which I had allowed to take possession of me. I must try to look on Ivers simply as a place where my great-grandmother had lived and which, inadvertently, had brought me a certain amount of fame and certainly not a little money. I ought, by rights, to be grateful to it. But how *could* I be? It was in this village that my only son had been killed, a village he would never have known, never gone to on that fatal night, but for me.

I climbed a stile and took the right of way up Hackpen Hill to Ivers Copse, just as I had once done with the Tanner family, more years ago than I liked to think about. I stood, for a while, looking down on the old grey stone house lying, amidst a riot of red and yellow dahlias, below me, its two huge oak trees still standing guard on either side. Was it just I, with my ridiculously over-active imagination, who had invented or, at any rate, read things into certain happenings which no one else would have thought twice about? There was nothing evil about Ivers, surely. The Tanners had found it a perfectly happy family home, as it must have been in Alice's day, that is, until her final years.

I let my eyes travel over the entire scene: the golden wheatfield in the foreground, the greeny-blue water-meadows below with, now and then, just a glint of silver where the sun shone on the river. The leaves of the trees had yet to fall, so that many a landmark was still obscured from view by copper beeches, elms with lemon patches, oaks tinged with a lighter yellow. But I could still pick out the tall chimneys of the Hall and the tower of the little Norman church, where I had diligently done some research, thanks to Alaric Reed.

It was all there, just as I remembered it. Then, suddenly, I was forced to put out a hand and steady myself on a fence post. There was one place I was glad I could not see, the place about which my great-grandmother had once written: *It's odd how unlucky that particular spot has always been.* I would make sure that Fred did not take me back by that route.

On reaching home, I decided not to mention the extra little peregrination I had made that day. It had not exactly harmed me, but had I been right to make it? I really didn't know, any more than I realised I didn't know very much about so many things. Advancing years were catching up with me fast. The urge to create now centred solely on my garden, which was practical and satisfying. But even over this I found myself going slower, sitting back and admiring, where once I would have been feverishly working.

It was one morning when I was doing just this, resting quietly on a seat in the shrubbery and looking at one of Robert's fields through a small vista I had made, that I heard the click of the wicker gate and turned to see Janet coming towards me.

'You have a visitor, Vicky,' she said. 'Someone you once spoke to me about.'

'Who?' I asked, puzzled.

'Gregory Fawcett.'

'Did you say where I was?'

'I said I'd go and look for you.'

There seemed nothing for it but to follow her back into the house.

I was ill prepared for the enormous, stooping, grey-haired figure who rose to meet me. Gregory might have been a complete stranger until he spoke. 'My *dear* lady,' he began, and I was once more back at the literary party where we had once met.

'I felt I had to call on you,' he went on. 'Your publishers didn't want to give me your address, but I wheedled it out of them in the end. You see, I've only *just* read *The Presentiment.* I can't think why I missed it when it first came out. I suppose I must have been abroad. Anyway, I found it riveting. It can't be true that you've written nothing since, surely?'

'Yes, it's quite true.'

'But, my *dear* lady, why? You can't let a talent like that go to waste.'

'I don't see why not,' I replied. 'Besides, I don't think I

believe in talent, Gregory. It was you yourself who told me that creative work had little or nothing to do with whomsoever actually executes it. You said it came from somewhere other and I think you're right.'

I gave him lunch, showed him round the garden and then, after he had gone, I went back to the shrubbery again. Anthony had made one of his rare visits to London and later on it would be time to meet his train but, just for now, I simply sat there, watching the sun sink lower in the sky, aware of the faint hum of a combine harvester in the distance, conscious that the warmer days were all but over. The seasons seemed to come round so quickly nowadays. It really *was* true that time passed more quickly as the years went by.

Time. My son, had he lived, would be getting on for forty. Janet's daughter even older. Why had we two mothers been spared and the young taken? Was there a plan? Who was to say? Frederick, with his surprising theory that life was so fleeting it hardly mattered when one died? Gregory Fawcett, with his confident belief in somewhere other? Anthony, with his mixture of scepticism and hope? And myself . . .?

I became lost in thought, so much so that I was startled to feel a hand on my shoulder. It was Janet, wisely and firmly bringing me back from the timeless moment with a reminder that I only had twenty minutes to get to the station.